"Duval?" the fellow was saying. "You mean Duval?"

"Do you know him?" she asked.

"Know him? Him with the pale face and the gray eyes?"

"Yes, yes, that's the man! You *do* know him?"

"Do I know him?" he said, releasing her arm—almost flinging it from him. "I know he's lower than a hound. I know he's a sneak and a skunk. I know enough to tell you about him."

Then his hand was filled with his gun. . .

Don't miss these other action Westerns by Max Brand from ACE CHARTER:

TWENTY NOTCHES
OUTLAW'S CODE
SAWDUST AND SIXGUNS
MONTANA RIDES
MONTANA RIDES AGAIN
THE REVENGE OF BROKEN ARROW
THE BORDER BANDIT

MAX BRAND
WRITING AS EVAN EVANS
STRANGE COURAGE

ACE CHARTER BOOKS, NEW YORK

STRANGE COURAGE
Copyright © 1930 by Dorothy Faust
Copyright renewed 1958 by Dorothy Faust

All rights reserved. No part of this book may be reproduced in any form or by any means, except for the inclusion of brief quotations in a review, without permission in writing from the publisher.

All characters in this book are fictitious. Any resemblance to actual persons, living or dead, is purely coincidental.

An ACE CHARTER BOOK

ISBN: 0-441-78856-4

First Ace Charter Printing: September 1982
Published simultaneously in Canada

Manufactured in the United States of America

2 4 6 8 0 9 7 5 3 1

STRANGE COURAGE

1

In the spring of the year Duval came to Moose Creek. Between the tall dark pines the underwoods were beginning to bloom with yellow-green as bright, well-nigh, as sunshine, and far away the dim avenues were streaked with color as though the sunlight had fallen through. On the hills, in the valleys, the cattle grazed, their sides hollow after the harsh winter. Cows bawled down the wind for their calves; the young bulls challenged the old masters with great bellowings; and in Moose Creek itself the screen doors were banging all day long as the children ran in and out from play. This was the season when Duval came down from the mountains.

It was old Simon Wilbur who saw him first.

Simon had gone hunting and his way had taken him up the weather-dimmed trail past his old place; he sat on the chopping block before the woodshed and, taking off his hat to the small breeze that managed its way through the forest, he saw Duval come up through the trees from the creek trail.

He was amazed. No one used that path in these days and had not for years; but presently he forgot the strangeness of the coming because of the way this man filled his eye.

Others later on were to feel the same thing, but though they were more talented in speech than Dad Wilbur, they had his trouble in putting a finger upon salient differences that distinguished Duval from other men. Certainly, from the limp brim of his hat to his spoon-handled spurs, he was dressed like any other cowpuncher of good taste; and as for his appearance, he was a sinewy man who had come to the full of his strength—but Simon Wilbur would not have bet on his age within five years. In fact there was nothing unusual about him, yet as Wilbur afterward expressed it, he felt at once that the stranger had "been around the corner and seen the other side."

"Hello," said Duval. "Now, this place I call something like."

"Like what?" said Simon Wilbur, who rarely committed himself in the most casual conversation.

Duval looked at the stout little cabin, the wood and horse sheds behind it, the two great trees which guarded the path to the water's edge, and the meadows that descended the hillside, still dotted with a few big stumps. The second growth saplings were coming up now, in clusters, but still the fields were fairly clear.

"That ground would raise crops, I lay my money," said he.

"It has," said Dad Wilbur.

"What sort of crops?" asked Duval. "Grain?"

"Rocks, mostly," replied Simon.

Duval laughed pleasantly, a rich laughter much deeper than his speaking voice.

"A fellow could work here, and be alone, too," said he. "How's the house?"

"You don't need a key to get in," said Wilbur.

Duval dismounted with a clinking of spurs and, after throwing his reins, went at once through the cabin. He looked out once from the attic window.

"This'd be tolerable warm in winter, partner," he called.

"Oh, it's warm enough," said Wilbur. "In summer, too!"

A little later, Duval came out again. This time he walked down to the creek and leaned there for a long moment against one of the great trees. The old path was quite grassed over now, except in the centre where many feet had worn through the surface soil to the gravel.

Then Duval turned on his heel.

"Who owns this outfit?" he asked.

"Why, stranger?"

"I'm fixed to buy, if it ain't the price of a summer resort or a dude ranch. What would Mister Real-estate Dealer say if I went and whispered in his ear?"

Simon Wilbur grew cautious.

"They's a house here," said he.

"Kind of mouldy, though," suggested Duval.

"They's some bang-up sheds, too, that cost a lot of makin'."

"They was made crooked, though," said Duval.

"And they's a hundred acres of land down there—"

"Fit to raise rocks, mostly," suggested the stranger.

Wilbur grinned in sympathy.

"I own this layout," he said. "Twenty dollars an acre ain't too much, and I'd throw in everything else for another thousand, and never bear you no hard feelin's because of your bargain."

"That's three thousand," observed Duval.

"You been to a right good school," said Wilbur.

"Sure I been to a good school," said Duval. "And after addition they taught us subtraction."

"What you gunna subtract?"

"Rocks," said Duval, "among other things. I'll pay you fifteen dollars an acre and take the buildings throwed in. That adds up to fifteen hundred. Do you like it?"

Wilbur raised his hands and his eyes to heaven, and sat as a picture.

"My name's Duval," said the other. "Do we shake on it?"

"Fifteen hundred!" said Wilbur. "Young feller, I like you. I like your cut and I even like your sassy way, but I'd hate to pay that much for a laugh. If I went home and faced Ma after makin' a deal like this—"

"She'd say she never knew you were a great businessman before. Look here. This land ain't been on the market because you didn't know there *was* a market. If I wasn't a doggone good man on a trail, I never would of tracked it down and got a chance to offer on it. Fifteen hundred dollars, and I leave it to you to fix the deed and the rest, or whatever you do when you buy land."

He took out a wallet from which he shuffled a number of notes, and displayed them to Wilbur.

"Two fives and four of a kind," said Duval, "is one better than a full house and would get you shot in parts of the country that I been in. Make your choice, mister. Will you play this hand? There ain't a second deal."

"I'll play this hand," said Wilbur, and took the proffered money.

"If you live near here and got a buckboard that I could borrow," said Duval, "I'd like to get down to town and buy some fixin's to go along with this roost."

Wilbur streaked down through the woods as fast as long old legs would carry him. Only when he came to his new home did he check his speed a little and, arriving at the back door, he spent a long time scraping his books on the iron that was fixed there.

"Is that you, Si?" called his wife. "If you ain't brought back some meat fit for lunch, you can get yourself downtown and fetch up some chops."

"I ain't got no meat," said Wilbur, "but I don't reckon that I'll be goin' downtown. I'm gunna drive the buckboard up to the old place."

"Are you gone crazy?" said she.

"No," said he, "I just give the place away, and now I'm gunna loan the young gent the buckboard."

The wife came rapidly down the steps and, taking him by the shoulders, looked earnestly into his face.

"You wo'thless old skinflint," she exclaimed. "What you been up to?"

"Givin' away the old place," he insisted, "and I got this in exchange."

Slowly, one by one, he took the notes from his pocket and spread them before her eyes.

"Lord God bless my soul," whispered Martha Wilbur. "Has somethin' worthwhile growed out of that place? You give him a promise to sell, wrote out, or something?"

"He didn't ask for nothin'," said he.

"Them that don't ask for bills of sale are them that don't need 'em," she decided. "Him that paid you that money once won't never pay it twice, Simon, and if you lied to him about the ground, you better be movin' to a new county over the hills!"

"I didn't lie," said Simon.

"Simon," she exclaimed, "I've lived with you nigh onto forty years!"

He seemed to accept the implication of this without resistance, but he added thoughtfully: "I didn't lie, because I couldn't. You'll know what I mean when you see him!"

2

Later in that same morning, Duval appeared in the town of Moose Creek itself, coming down the single street, until he reached Lane's Grocery Store.

At the hitching rack he tethered his team and went into the neatest mercantile interior that ever had graced Moose Creek. Linoleum was under his feet, its flowered pattern somewhat dim from vigorous scrubbing; all newly white-enamelled, the walls, the ceiling, and the shelves were shining; every jar of preserves stood in a strictly drilled line upon snowy oilcloth; the bins behind the counter for sugar, rice, beans, and flour carried not only their appropriate labels but like the walls were freshly coated with the same glistening paint.

A tall cowpuncher leaned at a counter toward the rear of the store, and he was the only human being Duval saw, at first. For the girl who stood opposite was in white also and lost against her background. She was stiffly done up in a long apron tied about her waist with a gigantic bow; she had great white cuffs and a broad collar of starched linen; in short, she was so extremely speckless and stood so stiff that Duval could have been excused for thinking her no more than a model or imitation of a pretty girl.

Now, however, she raised her eyes to the tall cowboy. Duval, even from the distance, could note two things: that she was saying "no," and that her eyes were blue.

Those eyes had opened so wide that she seemed to be listening rather than speaking, but the man who heard her voice snapped his fingers impatiently. He pushed the sombrero he was wearing far back on his head, which was covered with closely curling black hair.

"I've run uphill for six months, Marian, and I ain't gunna run no more," said he. "They's some that like huntin' for the sake of the walk and the fresh air, but I like the game that I kill. If you say 'no' now, it's final and for good. Y'understand that? Wait a minute. I—"

"Charlie, there's another customer—" she began.

"Damn the other customer," said Charlie. "Wait a minute and think. I've worked like Cain for six months. I've piled up a roll. The old man'll back me. I've got a place laidout . . ."

His excited voice sank out of hearing, not from caution or embarrassment, but with a profound emotion.

He ended and Duval, watching, waited to see compassion, pity, gentleness in the face of the girl, but he waited in vain. For again she looked up with the unmoved face of a doll, the big blue eyes opened: "No," said she.

The youngster who leaned on the counter did not wait for the end, neither did he say good-bye, but yanking his hat deep over his eyes, he turned on his heel and strode rapidly down the aisle toward Duval and the door. His black eyes glittered as they came, shining at Duval with a promise of trouble if there appeared in the stranger the slightest glimmer of a smile, the faintest suggestion of interest, of curiosity, of scorn.

But Duval already was reading the labels on the shelf!

He did not look down from his occupation until he heard her voice before him, asking what he would have. It was a small voice, high and sweet, like the voice of a child; and when he looked at her he saw that her hands were like the hands of a child also—softly dimpled across the knuckles.

Duval sat down on the high chair in front of the counter and took out a list.

"Here you are," said he. "I'm openin' up the old Wilbur place and it's a bare cupboard up yonder. I want it lined, and if I've forgotten anything, you fill it in, will you?"

She considered this appeal and the list at the same time, tapping the eraser end of a pencil against her chin.

It was a very complete list, she thought. She hoped that he would like the sort of bacons and hams that she carried. Did he care to see a sample of the flour? He did not!

From the corner of his eye, he looked through the broad front window of the store and saw young Charlie knock open the swinging door of Pete's Place, the saloon across the street. And Duval, looking back at the girl, caught the movement of her eyes by which he knew that she also had seen.

But not a shadow appeared in her face, not a tone of her voice altered. He determined to force the point.

"Listen!" said he. "It looks to me like your partner, Charlie, is gunna collect some trouble, the way he sashayed through that door across the street. I hope he's insured against broken glass, ma'am!"

She looked at him without the slightest emotion.

"A Nash is hard to break," said she. "Charlie is a Nash. I'll pick out the jellies and preserves. One glass of each kind until you've approved of them. Is there anything else? Or shall I start to fill the list?"

"A gent can't live on beef forever," said Duval, considering. "Lemme see. Between shifts some anchovies ain't so bad. Got any?"

"I can get anything you want—in a few days," said she, and looked up anxiously. Anxiety—for her business!

Duval raised his lean, pale face and looked through the window at the sky.

"Tarragon vinegar. Is that in your stock, ma'am?"

"I'll order that, too."

She was writing rapidly on a pad.

"And what about oil for salad. Real olive oil. Italian olive oil, please—"

He was conscious that she had stopped writing and was looking up from her pad at him with ever so slight a puckering of her eyes.

"And English mustard?" she asked. "And a few cloves of garlic?"

He met her eyes fully, and at once they opened wide, guileless as the glance of a child. But Duval had heard enough to make him rise at once from the chair and curse the moment he had entered that store.

"Yes," said he. "If you'll fill out that order, I'll drop in for it later on."

"Certainly," said she. "In twenty minutes, Mr.—"

"Duval," said he.

"Yes, Mr. Duval. As you go out, do notice our new line of brooms and mops. Brown and Hardy's line, and the very best. Anything in which I can serve you—in twenty minutes, Mr. Duval—"

She opened the door for him and smiled him out, a small, mechanical trade smile. And Duval found himself sweating on the sidewalk.

He turned up the street with long, slow steps, as one whose mind is profoundly occupied. He was heedless of the next two stores, but he turned in at the hardware shop, and then he sought the blacksmith's, where in the rear yard he wandered among rusty secondhand ploughs "better than new, because you can *see* what's the matter with 'em!"

"You're here to stay?" suggested the blacksmith.

"Unless they drive me out," said Duval, with the faintest of smiles, and sauntered easily down the street.

He was himself again, but he had arrived at one ardent conclusion. After this day, he would never again enter the grocery store and submit to the examination of the big, childish eyes of the girl in white.

So he went down to reclaim his groceries at the store; found them gathered near the door; paid the bill; bore them out to the waiting buckboard; and all without once meeting those blue, young eyes of the girl.

He had heaped his purchases into the tail of the wagon when the explosion occurred in Pete's Place across the street.

It was like an explosion in more ways than one. It was a series of reports accompanied by wild howls, crashings of glass, splinterings of wood, and then through the battered door of the saloon poured half a dozen men with the bartender last of all, his long white apron blown up by the wind of his running and streaming across his shoulder.

And as the bartender ran he was yelling: "Help! Get the sheriff! Help! Charlie Nash is loose agin!"

It was apparently a well-known name in Moose Creek. An echo of it ran up the street and down: "Charlie Nash!"

Doors slammed, feet rattled down steps, a crowd was rapidly pooling in a broad semicircle around the front of the saloon. No one occupied the center of the street, but the fringes were well filled. Men, women, children came out to listen to the blind show. For inside the saloon, glass still occasionally crashed, a revolver exploded, and some yet unbroken piece of furniture smashed.

"Poor Pete!" said a man near Duval. "He'll be ruined."

"Where is he now?" asked Duval.

The answer came at once, for a bottle flew through the gaping, broken windowpanes in front of the saloon, and was dashed to pieces in the road.

"He's busted into the cellar!" yelled the voice of Pete. "Ain't anybody gunna stop him? My God, I'm a ruined man! Ain't there any law? Ain't there any sheriff in this here county?"

"He ought to be stopped," remarked Duval to his neighbor.

"Sure he ought to," said the other drily. "Ideas is cheap, but they's a premium on bullet-proof men in this here town."

"He's most likely drunk," said Duval, "and couldn't shoot straight."

"That ain't the Nash way," said the other. "The more red-eye, the more they hit the bull's-eye."

"Do they?" said Duval and straightway turned and looked through the window of the grocery store.

He saw the girl within, not with hands clasped in terror and in horror, but mounted on a sliding ladder, stowing new jars in the dapper rows upon the shelves!

Duval smiled, but not with pleasure. He glanced around him at the gaping, uncertain faces of the crowd, then walked around its outskirts and straight up to the swinging door. Here he hesitated to pull his hat on more firmly.

"He's going in!" gasped someone, and a murmur repeated the phrase. "Follow him up! Come on, Buck, you and me!"

But no one stirred, and though Duval did not glance behind, he seemed to know that there was no help for him; so he pushed the door open, and stepped inside!

Those who waited in the street heard what they had expected—a rapid tattoo of gunshots, after that a thudding and crashing, then silence.

"He's dead, the poor fool!" said the blacksmith. "And I've lost the biggest bill that was ever ordered out of my shop. The poor sucker's been drilled in about twenty places."

"*I* told him," said another. "But he knew too much. Here's the sheriff. Hey, here comes the sheriff!"

The sheriff came on a running horse. He looked an imposing figure, with long sun-faded hair blown back over his shoulders and the brim of his felt hat furled by the wind of the gallop. But the moment he dismounted, throwing his reins at the same instant, he was revealed as a little bandy-legged man.

The blacksmith became the spokesman.

"Charlie Nash gets on a rampage, shoots up Pete's Place, smashes things a good bit, I guess. Along comes a stranger by name of Duval and walks in on him. I reckon you'll find Duval a dead man inside and Charlie gone off the back way, or else dead drunk."

The sheriff ran straight on toward the door of the saloon, but as he came closer the impetus of his resolution or of his sheer motion wasted away, so that he was walking only slowly when he came to his goal. There, however, he did not stop, but, drawing a revolver from the holster on his thigh, he threw the swinging door wide, and crouched to receive a shock.

What he saw made him straighten and run on into the place.

The sheriff appeared suddenly at the door again, with an odd expression of bewilderment and disbelief.

"Who's this Duval?" he asked. "Who *is* Duval?"

At this invitation, the entire crowd swayed in closer.

"A gent you won't forget once you've seen him," said the blacksmith. "The right kind of a lookin' man, sheriff. Ain't he on the floor in there?"

The sheriff stepped back.

"Come in and look!" said he.

They poured in willingly. The entire street emptied into Pete's Place where there was plenty to look at in the shape of shattered mirrors, smashed chairs and tables, bullet furrows in the ceiling and along the floor, but not a sign of the dead body of Duval.

They spread eagerly over the saloon and down into the cellar; they extended their search, shouting advice, opening every door, staring under beds, but still they found nothing, and gradually they flooded back into the main room of the saloon where Pete now stood again considering a little heap of seven hundred dollar bills, together with a brief note, which said:

> Sorry, Pete: If this ain't enough, let me know what else you want.
>
> Charlie.

The sheriff read this note and looked at the money, also. His bewilderment seemed to grow.

"I know Charlie and what Charlie can do!" said he. "I've seen enough examples of that. Didn't he gut this place and the seven men inside of it? But Charlie's gone! What did you hear when Duval came in?"

"Heard guns, then a crashing. Then nothin' at all."

The sheriff closed his eyes and furrowed his brow with intense thought.

"Duval comes in through the door; Charlie lets go at him. Duval dodges in close and takes the gun away from him—"

"Takes a gun away from Charlie Nash?" echoed Pete, aghast.

"Shut up!" said the sheriff. "I know it ain't possible. But I'm sayin' what must of happened! Takes the gun away from Charlie, and lays Charlie out cold on the floor. Then jerks him up to his feet, half sober. Shows him what he's done. Gets the money out of him. Writes the note for him—you see the writing ain't the same as the signature, don't you? Then shoves him out through the back door and gets him away!"

He paused and opened his eyes, looking around him dizzily.

"Where's Duval's hoss?"

"Out in the street. He come in with Dad Wilbur's buckboard."

So the sheriff went to the door, saying: "That'll be gone, by this time, and nobody'll know where it went!"

He was right, for when he threw the door open and stepped into the street, the buckboard had vanished. He went across to the grocery store and touched the brim of his hat to Marian Lane.

"You didn't see this stranger start, Marian?" he asked.

"I was busy in the store when he drove off," she said.

"When he drove off? Then you *did* see him?"

"I've an idea," said she, "that it wouldn't pay one to know too much about Mr. Duval!"

"Humph!" he grunted. "Marian, if that gent's come to stay, I want to get some information, and I know that you can get what you want out of a man. You start him talkin' the next time he comes in and I'll give you something to remember me by."

"Of course," said she, "I'll try to remember if I hear him talk, but I'm pretty sure that I'll never have a chance to talk with him again."

"Hey?" he barked at her. "Now whatcha mean by that, Marian?"

"Well," she answered thoughtfully, "the fact is that I don't think that he likes women very well."

"Is he as young as that?" grunted the sheriff, frowning.

"No, he's as old as that," she corrected. "What's happened to Charlie?"

"Been pulled out of the fire, thank God, by this Duval, from what I can make of it. But he ain't out of trouble yet. I'm gunna make this a lesson for him. It's jail for young Charlie for the disturbin' of the peace. Thirty days would do him a mighty lot of good!"

He watched the look of the girl wander askance toward a corner of the ceiling.

"You—Marian Lane!" he said sternly.

"Yes, Uncle Nat," said she.

"Will you wipe that baby look off of your face," he demanded, "and tell me out and out what you had to do with this here affair?"

"I? What could I have to do with it?"

"You, you!" he insisted. "What did you have to do with it?"

"I only know that Charlie was in here just before."

"What was Charlie tryin' to buy? You?"

She nodded, and the sheriff grunted with indignation.

"Takes his busted heart over to the saloon and smashes the furniture, eh? But I don't hardly blame him. If I was ten year younger, I suppose that you'd make *me* raise hell, too! Maybe thirty days is too long. Maybe a week would do, or just a talk from the judge."

He concluded solemnly: "Honey, what a terrible lot you got to answer for!"

"Dear Uncle Nat!" said she. "What have I to answer for?"

For reply, he strode with his odd waddle to the door, but there he lingered and finally turned back toward her again.

She stood with her hands clasped and her head hanging.

"You little wo'thless devil!" said the sheriff. "You knew that I'd turn around, and you wanted me to see a picture, didn't you? Anyway, honey, you ain't quite as bad as what I make out, maybe! Come over pretty pronto and pick yourself out a puppy. The brown bitch has a new litter."

He hurried out into the street, swung into the saddle, and was stopped by Pete, who ran hastily out to him.

"If you give Charlie a runnin' for this job," said Pete, "he'll sure murder me. Leave him be, won't you?"

"I never lay no whip on a free puller," grinned the sheriff. "Don't you worry too much about what I'll do to Charlie, but think a mite about what he's likely to do to me. Howsomever, I can't lay down and let such things as this happen in the town, can I? Get up, Buck!" He spoke to the horse, touched it with his spur, and instantly was at full speed out of the town and up the hill that led toward the old house of Simon Wilbur.

3

So Sheriff Nat Adare came to the lower meadows of the old Simon Wilbur place, and riding across these, he came to the front door of the cabin. A fragrance of cooking meat blew out to him, and the sheriff found himself a very hungry man. He dismounted, tethered the horse, and knocked at the door.

It was opened to him at once by the stranger.

He never had seen the man before, never had heard the pale face described, and yet he knew with a perfect certainty that this was Duval. Someone had said that, once seen, he never could be forgotten, or words to that effect, and the sheriff knew that it was true.

"You're Duval?" he said at once.

"And you're Sheriff Adare?"

"D'you know me, young feller?"

"As well, I reckon, as you know me, sheriff. Will you come in?"

"I figgered on doin' that," nodded the sheriff.

"Bring your hat along with you," said Duval, failing to move from the doorway, "but we got a rule here that visitors hang their guns outside."

He pointed to half a dozen new, large nails

which had been driven recently into the logs beside the door, and the sheriff considered them for a moment as though he were reading a page of print.

"Most generally," he observed, "I aim to carry my guns with me. It's kind of a rule in my business."

"Why," said Duval, "likely it is, but it never does a gun no harm to get a lot of fresh air."

Nat Adare hesitated an instant longer, then obediently unbuckled his gun belt and hung it on the first nail.

"Come in," said his host genially. "You're in time to have chow with me, sheriff."

"Thanks," said the sheriff. "I don't mind if I do. Am I smellin' venison or dreamin' by day?"

"This here?" said Duval innocently. "Why no! This here is something that I bought at the butcher's."

"Humph," said the sheriff, and stepped through the door.

He saw that the place suddenly had become habitable. Two or three old, broken chairs had been revamped. The little table no longer staggered on three legs, and in the corner of the room the old stove which the Wilburs had abandoned as past all use had been made to support a roaring fire.

"Why, partner," said the sheriff, "you must have somebody already with you."

He pointed at the two places which were set out on the table.

"It's an old rule in my family," said Duval, "never to set down without layin' an extra plate. It's more sort of companionable, sheriff!"

"The same gent in your family fixed that rule that made the one about guns and fresh air, I s'pose?"

"The same one. Dad was a great hand for rules, and mostly I find they come in handy. Gimme your hat. That's the best chair over yonder. I'll fix you a basin of hot water if you'll wash your hands. And can I put up your hoss and give him a feed of oats?"

"Thanks," said the sheriff, sniffing again the fragrance of the cookery, and scanning the simmering coffeepot, the frying pan from which the rankness of cooking onions steamed forth, and other bubbling pots which made music, all in varying keys. "Thanks, Duval, but I don't take off my hat in no man's house until I've had a chance to speak my business. I don't eat salt and meat unless . . ."

He paused, and looked straight at his host.

"Duval, what happened down there in the saloon?"

"Saloon?" said Duval, in polite inquiry.

"What did you do to young Nash in Pete's Place?"

"Ah, yes," said Duval, recalling himself. "When I sashayed in there, I expected to have a handful of trouble, but the fact is there wasn't any at all!"

"Humph!" said the sheriff. "Duval, was Nash there?"

"Perhaps he was," said Duval. "I dunno, exactly. I was sort of flustered and nervy, just then."

"Guns went bangin' after you entered," observed Adare.

"Yes, they did," said Duval. "The fact is that I wanted Charlie Nash to know that I was comin' along, and if he had any idea of gettin' out by the back door, that would be a good signal for him."

"Who wrote the note that Charlie left behind him?" demanded the sheriff.

"That's a thing that I dunno as I could say," replied the host. "Set down, sheriff. I dunno that any man gets very far by just standin' around!"

The point of this remark made Adare grin broadly.

"There ain't anybody else in this house, I s'pose?" said he.

"It was a rule of my old man," said Duval, "never to lock no doors and windows. Locked doors keep the air out and the smoke in, he used to say. Maybe you've heard that sayin', sheriff?"

"I dunno that I have. Your old man must of been a rare one, eh?"

"The finest in the world," said Duval. "Hosses was his main hold, but he wasn't so bad with men, neither. He was full of ideas, but mostly he said that them that wanted to get along in the world had better keep their own floor swept and not mind about the neighbors."

The sheriff winced a little, but then broke out into frank laughter.

"Son," said he, "I like the way that you go about things. Who are you, Duval?"

"Me? Why, just an ordinary cowhand, sheriff. Got a little stake and come along through the hills lookin' for a place to set up farmin'."

"Bein' off the main highroad don't depress you none, I guess," said Adare.

"The old man always said," was the answer, "that a mite of solitude done a lot for a man's nerves."

"You don't look nervous, Duval!"

"Don't I? I'm mighty glad of that. But I been reckoned a tolerable nervous man, Adare."

The sheriff smiled again.

"Duval," he said, "where you been?"

"Me? Up at the T Bar talkin' to the cows, walkin' in the mud, and gettin' up at about four-thirty in the mornin's."

"What made you quit? Or was you fired?"

"I quit, because God don't make a long enough day to suit the boss of the T Bar, and has to piece out with lantern light."

"I seen them kind of bosses," agreed the sheriff with enthusiasm. "Doggone their ornery hides!"

The sheriff threw his hat in the corner and suddenly sat down.

"Call in Charlie Nash!" said he. "Call in Charlie and be damned, you lyin', four-flushin', two-legged maverick."

And as the rear door of the shack opened, Charlie Nash appeared with a wash basin in his hands.

"Why, hullo, Nat," said he. "When I get some hot water into this basin, it'll be about right for you to rub some of the harness blackin' off of your hands. How are you, old-timer?"

The sheriff looked without malice on the youth. A handsome lad was Charlie Nash and looked the part for which he was given credit around the town of Moose Creek, and over all the broad county thereabouts. For it was said that Charlie Nash could drink more, fight harder, and lift a bigger weight than any man on the range. Supple, thick-chested, straight-eyed, he was one to have raced for a prize, or fought for it.

He was marred in one place, however, for the keen eye of the sheriff found a slightly purple swelling just to the side of the square point of Charlie's jaw.

Charlie Nash, unabashed, noted the direction of

the sheriff's glance, and nodded as he put down the basin.

"Sure," said he. "That's the place where he turned out the light. Step up, Nat. There's the soap, and here's a towel."

The sheriff rose, bent over the basin and liberally soaped his hands, his face, until the bristling eyebrows were a fluff of snow, his neck, until the suds filled the seams that checked it. He talked explosively between rubs.

"Now, boys," said he, "I'm in your hands. You been and made a fool of yourself, Charlie. And maybe I'm makin' a fool of myself up here."

Here the host broke in quietly: "I reckon that you're wrong about that, sheriff!"

"Why, it's kind of likely that I am," replied Nat Adare. "The way that I figger it, you're sorry for that fracas, Charlie. Besides, I know what started it."

He turned from the basin, dripping water on the floor and glaring at Charlie.

Charlie merely grinned.

"You can talk right out," said Charlie. "He knows what started it, too!"

"I reckon, Charlie," said the sheriff, "that you'll go back with me, and while I sit on my hoss with my guns buckled on, lookin' plumb wild, you'll make a speech to the boys and tell 'em how sorry you are that you have been a jackass, but the sheriff is gunna give you another chance after you've paid for the harm you done to Pete. And then you'll buy a drink all around!"

"Make a talk like that—" began Charlie Nash, in great excitement. "I'd rather—"

"Sure you'd rather," said the host gently. "The

old man used to say that the first speech was the first step up the ladder in politics, and it never made any difference what the speech was about!"

4

Sooner or later all the chief men of Moose Creek went up to call on Duval; the more daring spirits among the boys used to venture there also, and they found him ploughing with a team made up of his saddle horse and an old brown mule he had bought from old Wilbur. Of the evenings, it was known that he kept Monday for laundry work and for the repairing of his clothes, but the other nights of the week he was glad to have visitors. They would come and find him beside a circular lamp with a green shade, reading, and whoever arrived was certain of a welcome. He never was at any labor so important that he would not pause from it and invite the guests to sit on his veranda, if the day were fine, and drink some of Pete's best beer, which was constantly kept cooling in the icy water of the creek; this, with sausage sliced delicately thin, or cheese of a quality unheard of before in Moose Creek, made repasts to be talked of long afterward.

Sometimes late-callers in the afternoon were asked to stay on for supper, which Duval prepared like a chef. He could make a man at home in one moment; his pale face was so full of courteous attention, and his gray eyes dwelt so carefully on every word that each man felt he had been selected from many and placed high in the consideration of the new resident. There were two extra beds, also, which frequently were filled, and it might be said that no man in Moose Creek lived with less real privacy than Duval. It became known that he was a thoroughly good fellow. He would go down to Pete's Place and drink his beer or his red-eye, up to a certain point, with any man; and if the other fellow's pocket were emptied, Duval never permitted a scarcity of drink, for all of that. Within ten days it would have been safe to say that he had become the most popular man in the district.

Yet no one knew much about him. He talked freely of his garden, his farm, his work, his house; but he never chatted of his past beyond his days on the T Bar ranch, where the boss thought that Providence had not furnished our earthly laborers with enough hours of daylight for their work.

No one, moreover, could persist with the questioning of Duval past a certain point. It was not that his exploit in the saloon with Charlie Nash had given him a formidable reputation, for he was always the soul of good nature and gentleness, but behind the good nature there appeared that quality of secret strength which Moose Creek saw and appreciated but could not define.

His peculiarities of behavior were few, but they were pointed. He kept close to his work, rarely going out except to Pete's Place for an hour of an evening, now and then. He no longer came down to do shopping but old Wilbur was paid to stop by every day on his way to shopping. Whatever Duval needed was written down on a list, and this Wilbur carried from store to store and brought back the needed articles in the evening. Neither did Duval ever go to the post office, for no mail ever arrived for him, a fact which the postmistress commented on at some length! Women, too, it was known he despised. He could be lured out to visit a bachelor's house if only men were there.

However, men do not object to a companion whose interest is not in the other sex. The peculiarities of Duval were to his honor. They increased his dignity and fortified his position in the community.

It was not from Duval that they learned the first bit about his unknown past; it was from chance.

In that chance, as in the first instance when he appeared in Moose Creek, there appeared Marian Lane and Charlie Nash and Pete's Place. There also appeared a stranger.

Now, on this evening, the stranger came into the store and, like Duval on the first occasion, he found the girl talking with tall Charlie Nash. His fine fury, of course, had died long ago, and he had come humbly back with apologies and regained as much of a place with her as he ever had attained.

"Dear Charlie," she said to him this evening, "why do you waste so much time on me?"

"Because some day," said Charlie Nash, "you're gunna light up, and I want to be on hand to see the fire! Ain't that a good reason?"

This he said as the door opened, and the stranger came in. It was a very dark evening, the sky being covered with low clouds that shut away the last light of the sun and made a lamp necessary in the store.

"Gimme some canned tomatoes," said he, "and

make it pronto. I'm rushed."

"Oh, yes," said Marian Lane. "For mulligan?"

"Yes," he said. "Mulligan. The damn hotel is filled up! There ain't any other place in the town where a white man can stay! But it ain't the first time that I've made home in a 'jungle'!"

Charlie Nash stood up from his counter-chair and regarded the new man carefully. One does not swear in the presence of a girl in the West; certainly not of a stranger.

But this fellow was one who apparently made his own rules of conduct, wherever he went. His skin looked like brown leather, a little red-tinted over the bridge of the nose and across the cheekbones. He had a lipless mouth with a hook at one sde of it, and eyes so filled with evil that they were unashamed of showing it.

"Well, I'll tell you," said Marian. "We have a very hospitable fellow who lives just out of town. He might take you in."

"I don't go battering doors for a bed," said the other ungratefully. "A hoss blanket and a swiped chicken and a can of tomatoes will make me a supper anywhere, and a bed after it."

"Oh, but you wouldn't have to beg!" said she. "Mr. Duval—"

The other reached a gloved hand across the counter with no hurry, but with inescapable speed. It settled on her arm and held her as though he feared that she would escape.

Charlie Nash doubled his fist and came cautiously nearer. But down this traveller's right thigh was buckled a long holster out of whose top there blossomed the handle of a full-grown Colt forty-five. And Charlie was not carrying a gun. It was an act of penance to which Duval had persuaded him after the almost fatal incident in Pete's Place.

So Charlie hesitated.

"Duval?" the fellow was saying. "You mean Duval?"

"Do you know him?" said she.

"Know him? Him with the pale face and the gray eyes?"

"Ah, that's the man!" she admitted. "You *do* know him?"

"Do I know him?" he said, releasing her arm—almost flinging it from him. "I know he's lower than a hound. I know he's a sneak and a yaller skunk. I know enough to tell you about him. Where's his house?"

"Stranger," said Nash. "That there is a friend of mine. I don't allow no—"

He almost ran his nose into the end of a levelled gun. It came so suddenly that Charlie hardly had time to realize the seriousness of his position, but rolling his eyes in amazement, he saw Marian Lane exhibiting neither fear nor horror, but merely watching with a rather critical curiosity.

That was for Charlie Nash almost as great a shock as the gun in his face.

"Fill your hand and *then* talk to me about your friends!" snarled the big man.

"I ain't heeled," declared Charlie, "or you wouldn't have caught me cold."

"You lie," said the tall man. "You're a sneak and a liar like your friend Duval, that murders and then sneaks away out of the trouble that he's got comin' to him! I know you, boy!"

"Yonder," said Charlie with quiet fierceness, as though he could keep his words from reaching the ears of the girl on the other side of the counter, "is the only good saloon in Moose Creek. It's Pete's Place. You go in there and tell Pete that I sent you. He'll feed you the best in the place."

"And you?" asked the other, gradually recovering the gun, and finally dropping it into a holster.

"I'll pay the bill," said Charlie Nash, "after I've gone home for my gun and come back and laid you out. I'll pay for your drinks, and they'll be the last that you'll lap up around here, old son!"

The other patted the butt of his Colt and nodded with an ugly smile that was almost approval.

"I like to hear 'em talk up," said he. "How long will you be gone?"

"Twenty minutes—a half-hour—not more!"

"I'll wait for you," said the tall man. "I'll have you first, and your friend afterward. Ma'am, I've changed my mind about havin' tomatoes!"

He left the can on the counter, unpaid for, and strode through the doorway to the street.

"You'd better hurry, Charlie, if you want to get home and back in twenty minutes," said Marian Lane.

He started from his dream and glared at her.

"What's in you, Marian?" he demanded of her. "What's wrong with Duval that you mention his name to every gent that comes this way? What's he done that you should have it in for him? Confound me if you ain't the bottom of all the trouble that I have in this town!"

5

When Charles Nash had left, running like a man pursued through the door, the girl waited for another moment, then acted swiftly. She locked the front door of the shop, pulled down the lamp on its chains until she could extinguish it, and then ran back through the aisle of the store, swerving this way and that in the darkness to avoid every obstacle.

She opened a rear door that led to her own rooms above, and fleeing up the stairs, she was plucking off white apron and white dress as she went.

Quickly she dressed, then down the stairs she went, swinging herself through the doorway at the bottom by one hand, like a fugitive boy with a father's wrath behind him—so raced outdoors.

Behind her store was a small corral where one little-used pinto grew fat and sleepy, day by day, but now that his mistress came in dire need of him, he frisked at once to life, and scurried from corner to corner in the corral, throwing up his heels, and grunting with content at this pleasant excitement.

He was dragged in by the mane, saddled, bridled, and she was in the saddle.

She did not go up the main street of the town. It was her purpose to remain unseen, in all that followed, if she could manage it—unseen except by one pair of eyes; so she took the way she knew across the back lots, dodging here and there behind the back fences, stooping to keep from being knocked from her place by the low boughs.

In this way she came out upon the highroad that climbed the hill, but even this she did not follow, preferring to plunge straight across it and take the dim trail by the bank of the creek. This was daring riding.

When they reached ploughed ground, it checked the pony so suddenly that she was nearly flung from the saddle, but she recovered in time to check him just beneath the house.

There she dismounted and threw the reins; there for a moment she waited, breathing deep, replacing her hat in its proper position, relaxing from the strain of the gallop. Then she went to Duval's door.

The evening was warm. A shower in the afternoon had purified the air without chilling it, and therefore the door was open, so that she could look in on Duval beside his green-shaded light. She had heard other men describe the details of his household appointments so carefully that she knew them now as though her eye already had rested on them.

She saw the stove, the top of it carefully scrubbed clean of soot and grease stains—that famous stove on whose naked, glowing iron Duval cooked his famous steaks. She saw wood for the next fire stacked neatly at one side, the kindling in a tidy pile near it; the table on which those celebrated feasts were spread divided the room in two, as it were. The part nearest the door was kitchen and dining room. Beyond stretched the circular rag rug, rich with red and blue. A shelf of books filled a corner; why had no one told her of their titles? Three or four big, comfortable chairs; a little round table with a lamp on it, the green-shaded lamp, and the pale face of Duval lost in shadow, the light falling only on his open book, and the lean hands which held it.

She saw this in that instant she paused at the door, and knew that Duval had become aware of her before he lowered the book and looked up.

Now that the book was down, he came to her hurriedly.

"You ain't come sashaying all the way up here through the night, have you?" asked Duval. "Not on account of that tarragon vinegar? That could of waited, even if Dad Wilbur did ask for it again today."

"Why," said she, "it wasn't the tarragon." She drawled the words carefully. "It was a bit of news that I thought you ought to hear. News about a friend of yours."

"What friend?" asked Duval.

"Charlie Nash. A stranger came into the store this evening and happened to hear your name—"

"From you?" asked Duval mildly. But she felt the keen gray eyes fixed on her steadily.

"I don't remember—Charlie, I think. It seemed to throw the man into a state—a big, lean, ugly man, with a leathery face, and a crooked thin mouth. He wanted to know where you live and he said such things about you that Charlie—"

"Tackled him?"

"Ran straight into a gun."

"And Charlie's bare-handed!" said Duval. "Bare-handed, on account of my advice—"

"The stranger is waiting for him now in Pete's Place," she ended. "He'll be down there in five minutes, or so, I expect. Charlie will, I mean!"

Duval reached a hat from a peg on the wall.

"You rode up?" he asked in his gentle way.

"Yes," she said.

"I reckon you won't mind walkin' back, then," said Duval. "I'm kind of pressed for time."

He was through the door as he spoke; she, following a step or two, was in time to see him spring on the back of Pinto like a mountain lion at the kill, heard the grunt of the pony as strong knees crushed its sides, then the scuffling of hoofs that struggled for a footing in the loose earth, and horse and rider vanished in the gloom.

She started a step or so after him, but, reconsidering, she went hurriedly back into the house, and stood before the books.

They were battered volumes. A worn set in blue buckram bindings was labelled with the title *Hakluyt's Voyages;* she saw *Tom Jones* in two fat volumes; there was a narrow Marlowe beside it, then a book on woodland flowers, one on the game fishes of Catalina Island; Boccaccio wickedly sat in a dark corner.

She had seen enough titles, and hurrying toward the door she only paused to glance at the thick volume he had been reading as she entered. *It* was the most self-revealing, the wisest of essayists, Montaigne.

"Cowpuncher my foot!" said she. "But what *is* Duval?"

She carried that question unanswered into the

open night, then remembered the thing that might be happening even this moment in the village of Moose Creek.

That thought started her running, light as a boy, with a swiftly springing step, straight down through the perils of the dark creek trail.

She knew every feature of the place out of the exploits of her childhood, which had ended not so many years before. She could lead the way into perilous adventures in the times when she wore overalls, a flipping pigtail stuffed inside her jacket most of the time, and knees as often bruised and gashed as those of any headlong boy in Moose Creek. And still, at times, she yearned for the years when she had worn her freckles with never a care in the world.

The old practice was gone, but still she knew how to climb up the brick wall that helped to keep the river at bay from the rear marches of Pete's back yard. The top of it was not four inches wide, and there was a long fall to the water beneath, yet she stood upright, and walked easily along it, her arms stretched out on either side to give her balance.

She reached the rear wall of the house. On its roof she once had hidden in an important crisis of a game of hide-and-seek, to the despair of every boy in the village. Now she worked her way deftly across it, lowered herself to the low top of the kitchen, and from this dropped again to the ground.

She was inside the back yard of Pete's Place, without the use of a key for entering that sanctuary.

And straight before her was an open window

that allowed fresh air to blow in among the billows of smoke that filled the bar-room.

The big stranger was nearest to her. She could have reached through the window and touched his shoulder. Beyond him stood half a dozen others with tall beer glasses before them, or little whisky glasses, no taller than three of her slender fingers. Those who stood farthest from her were dimly seen through the haze of smoke from burning cigarettes. But Duval was not there!

She rubbed her eyes like a child wakening from sleep and looked again, searchingly, into every corner.

It was true: Duval had not come!

Hurriedly she strove to reconstruct or to adapt her conception of the man, but no matter what shadows she could admit into the picture, she could not think of him as one tainted by cowardice. Yet, when she looked again at the stranger, she was not so sure, for he seemed to Marian Lane the most formidable creature she had ever seen.

He stood now in an attitude of reflection at the bar, which Pete polished solicitously before him.

"I seen you before, stranger, I reckon?" suggested Pete.

"No," said the other, "you never did, or you'd know me. I'm Larry Jude. There's one around here that's called a man," went on Jude. "Duval!"

Pete stood stiffly at attention.

"You know his house?"

"Yes," said Pete.

"Man!" repeated Jude. "Boy-killer, I'd say!"

It was a fierce hour of trial for Pete. He grew pale, but he did not go back on his duty to a friend.

"He's pretty high considered around here," said

he. "He—he's a friend of mine, in fact."

"A friend of yours?" said Jude. "A friend of yours?"

His great shoulders swayed a little forward over the bar; but Pete stood his ground, very white of face now. Jude, however, suddenly laughed.

"A boy-killer is what I said. A boy-killer! D'you hear me? D'you all hear me when I talk?"

He threw up his head, and every man at the bar started. Yet they kept their attention, in pretense, fixed upon their drinks, so that it was obvious that they did not wish to have attention specially focused upon them.

The girl at the window, no matter what her excitement, scanned these faces critically and knew that she would remember them as men who had failed, for there was not one of these, she was sure, but had accepted the hospitality of Duval either in his house or at this bar, or had listened to his singing and praised it, or won from him deeply at cards, or "borrowed" a stake to take himself home.

She was hardly amazed when she saw them turn their heads from Jude toward the other end of the bar; for certainly they would have chosen to find another object of interest in that direction.

In fact, she did actually discern a new form just against the farther window. She could not see the face, but she made out the leisurely posture of the figure, one elbow on the bar and the hands loosely interlocked. Then, as by a single phrase one recognizes a piece of music, so she recognized Duval!

How he had come, she could not tell. There had been no noticeable swinging open of the door, but like a ghost he had melted into this room and materialized at the bar facing Jude.

She glanced back at that lofty man, and saw that from the moment of throwing up his head he had not stirred, except his right hand, which gripped the handle of his Colt. Powerfully he gripped it, the skin whitening over the knuckles; but except for that sign, he looked rather like a soldier, frozen in the attitude of attention.

So were they all, for that matter, from Pete to the least of the drinkers at his bar—one with glass arrested halfway to his lips, one with a match flaming in his fingertips but never approaching the cigarette for which it was intended, all of them men of stone except that insouciant figure at the farther end of the bar.

He who held the match had his fingers singed, and started as he dropped the red ember; at that movement the gun of Jude leaped almost from its holster—then slowly sank back again into the leather, and all the line at the bar slipped away, softly, as though they would not attract attention, and flattened themselves against the wall.

Their heads never had turned; at big Jude they cast not a single look but kept their attention riveted upon Duval. She herself could hardly draw her eyes away until, as a rift opened in the smoke, she saw that he was smiling.

At this, with a gasp, she glanced back at Jude to see how he was taking it. First she noted that the hand which grasped the Colt was trembling; and then she discovered that his coat across the shoulders was growing slack and tense in turns as he drew in great breaths. His head, indeed, moved a little with the greatness of his breathing. So Jude was struggling. He was able and willing enough to risk his life in quick action, she could have wagered, but this slow torment, this mysterious strain of nerves and will against an intangible force was breaking him.

He shuddered, suddenly, from head to foot. She could see his jaw sag and his tongue moisten his lips.

At that moment Duval spoke; the sound of his voice made the gun leap again in the holster of Jude, but for the second time he failed to draw it clear; there was a different reason now, she could guess.

"And here's another Jude!" Duval had said.

He walked slowly down the bar-room with his hands resting lightly on his hips—far, far from any weapon. Indeed, if he were armed, there was no sign of it. She did not notice, as she wondered at the super-human courage of this man, how he was dressed. Details of his appearance had not struck her eye when she saw him in his house, but now she was aware of blue overalls gathered about the hips with a tanned belt of common hide, and of a flannel shirt that once had been blue but was faded almost gray from the wash tub. It was open at the throat and the sleeves were rolled up to the elbows for comfort and coolness, no doubt, but in part one would guess because the sleeves had shrunk.

As he came, the enchanted eyes of the watchers followed him; big Jude shrank back perceptibly until his shoulders were pressed against the window and obscured her vision.

She could only hear the voice of Duval speaking terrible things in the most casual tone!

"If I'd had an idea there was more like the kid," said Duval, "I wouldn't have knocked him over to stop him; I would have killed him, partner. But I figgered that he was the only one of his kind and that maybe the world wouldn't want to lose him. He'd do behind bars to be looked at, five cents a look. But now that I have a slant at you, I know it's a tribe, like the snake tribe, all poison and no use, except they eat rats and toads, and such."

The voice grew very near. Fascinated, and with mounting tension in her heart, she saw the big shoulders of Jude strain still farther back.

"But you've come huntin' in the wrong place, Jude. Here in Moose Creek we don't keep rats and toads even to feed the Judes with. You'd starve here, partner. So leave your teeth behind you and —get out!"

Jude did not stir.

"D'you hear?" said Duval. "Drop your gun belt, and move!"

There was a heavy clatter on the floor.

Then she could see Jude stumbling toward the distant door with the back of one hand raised across his eyes as though he wished to cover his shamed face from the sight of men.

He shrank cowering to one side, and then ran— fairly ran! In his blindness he struck the doorjamb, staggered, and then pitched forward into the street with both his arms cast out before him as though the darkness were more precious than all the treasures of the world.

She did not go at once, partly because she was too weak to move from her supporting hold on the window-sill, and partly because an unhealthy fascination kept her there to look once more on Duval and wonder again who he could be, and what. She had seen murder done in the streets of Moose Creek. She had heard men scream and pray and watched them fight for breath—ay, and when she was only a child; but this was worse than murder that she had seen this night. Murder slays the body, but Duval had dared to put out his hands and lay them on a man's soul.

He did not allow the grisly suspense to end in any depressing aftermath, but waved the spectators forward to the bar.

"We need to drink together friends," said he. "And you with us, Pete. I wanta thank you!"

He reached his hand across the bar and gripped the most willing hand of the bartender.

"I should of said more," said Pete honestly. "I *tried* to say more for you, but I was plumb scared and couldn't choke out the words. D'you hear me, partner?"

"I waited out there beyond that window and watched and listened, mighty scared myself, until I seen that all of you boys was behind me!"

She who eavesdropped pressed her hands suddenly together, for she had wondered how he could do this thing and rescue the self-respect of the loungers in the room. But he had done it!

He was stretching out both hands and gripping theirs.

"Good old Jerry. When I seen you, Mike, it give me a lot of heart; and old Sam wouldn't let me down, I was right sure, nor Josh, nor Cap Sloane, and Bud Granger never said no to a friend!"

He stood by the bar and with a tender eye embraced their foolish, grinning faces. They began to praise themselves for their great courage, their dauntless bearing—these sheep!

Only Pete, who had dared to speak for his absent friend in the moment of need, now sat on a whisky keg with his face in both hands, trembling.

"One of you come and pour the drinks," he said. "I'm tuckered out. I feel right bad. My God, Duval, how glad I was when I seen you come in, but how scared, too!"

With a warm rush of emotion Marian said to herself that Pete was too good a man to be bartender in Moose Creek, or in any other town!

The street door was cast open again; and this time young Charlie Nash came into the room highheaded, bright of eye, like a thoroughbred groomed for a race, and expecting one.

"It ain't over, yet, is it?" he cried, "That—that thing that I passed slumpin' down the street—that wasn't *him,* was it?"

They hailed him with a joyous shout as Jerry poured the second round and assured him that it was indeed "him," and the him was none other than Larry Jude. But the master had met him, and faced him, and crushed him!

She saw Charlie Nash brush them aside and confront Duval.

"How did you do it, Duval?" he asked. "How did you do it, David?"

The girl, listening, was oddly startled to hear that word; for some absurd reason it seemed out of place for Duval to have a first name like other men.

"All I know," said Duval in his quiet way, "is that he was here, and now he ain't. But how it happened, I dunno."

"He stood up there at the end of the bar—" began Jerry.

Duval raised a hand that stopped this rehearsal.

"Well, boys, drink hearty. Step up, Charlie, boy! Jerry, come here!"

He drew Jerry aside, close to the window. She heard him say: "Don't take money for these drinks. But keep a reckoning, and let me know what it comes to, will you?"

"Chief," said Jerry, "what you say is all the law that I want for what's right and what's wrong! Hey, boys, drink up, and have another."

"Let everybody that comes in have what he wants," said Duval. "Bottoms up, boys. Good luck all round! Who can start us a song? You, Mike! Start us a chorus, will you?"

The song began with a rouse; it rose to a roar; and when Marian Lane looked again, she saw that newcomers were surging through the street door to join the fun. But the whole aspect of the crowd had changed, unknown to itself. For Duval was gone!

Now it was simply a confused and stupid drunken party, and she hurried away with a sense of shame that she had remained so long. It was not so easy to go as it had been to enter. In the other days, when she wore overalls like the boys of the town, she had been able to swing herself lithely up from the ground to the projecting kitchen eaves, and from the kitchen roof to that above. But now it was a great strain.

Twice she failed in her first effort and then, resting, panting, she looked up to the broad, bright face of the heavens and told the stars that she was not half of what she once had been.

This touch of scorn seemed to nerve her; the third attempt was successful, and thereafter she rapidly gained the upper roof, stole along the gutter to the place above the wall, and lowered herself to it.

She dared not walk boldly along it now, however, as she had done in coming. Something had gone from her in the meantime, and she had to crawl on hands and knees, gritting her teeth with self-contempt the while.

A moment more and she had dropped down outside the wall.

It was not until she had actually made a pace that she realized someone was standing before her, almost lost in the darkness of the trees—someone who must have been there all during the time she scrambled down the wall and then rested against it.

A scream leaped into the throat of the girl and died behind her set teeth. The impulse to run merely made her sway and was equally mastered. Yet she could not help drawing back from him, though Duval was no giant, and she knew it was he!

"Yes, sir," drawled the voice of Duval, "doggone me if it ain't hard to find a quiet place for a stroll, around Moose Creek."

"You saw me through the window!" she declared. "But you *couldn't* have seen my face."

"There wasn't nothin' to that," he said. "But I thought that I seen something like a khaki sleeve and figgered it might be you. So I brung around the hoss to give it back to you. And thanks a lot, Miss Lane."

He tugged at something—and there came the pinto, which had been standing all this time beneath the trees, at the end of the long reins.

"Them that start out on hossback hadn't ought to come back on foot," said Duval gently, "just because they loaned a hoss to a friend. Good night, ma'am!"

"Duval!" she called to him as he turned away. "Mr. Duval!"

He came back to her at once, though still keeping his distance. It was hard to talk to him; but she felt that this was the time to make an effort.

"You waited for Charlie. Was that it?" she asked him.

"Why," said the drawling voice, "it was kind of partly that I didn't want Charlie bustin' into my party, and partly that I wanted to size up Jude through the window. It ain't an easy thing to be throwed into the ring with a gent whose style you don't know."

She knew it was not true, but, as appeared to be the rule with him, he was hiding his real scorn of all other men beneath an apologetic manner. From the same source had sprung his desire to put the men of the barroom at their ease and recall their self-belief.

Then all the other questions which had been brooding in her mind, not yet come to words, drew back, and became more nebulous than ever. She knew that he had erected a wall between them, and she said simply: "Good night, Mr. Duval."

Yet, as he went off through the night, there was fierce indignation rising in her. He had feared her because she had seen a little through him and his disguise that day in the store; if he despised her now in her new role as eavesdropper, she bitterly resolved to make him change his mind.

6

It is true that one good action will establish a Westerner for life. But two such actions, in one small town, under the eyes of one audience, were more than enough to place Duval upon a pedestal. With the exception of Marian Lane, who had no confidants, probably there was not a soul who felt that there was anything evil in the power of Duval. He had picked young Charlie Nash out of the slough and set him on the high road; he had met the juggernaut, Larry Jude, and crushed him in the palm of his hand.

Besides, he minded his own affairs, but was willing to listen to those of others. He worked hard, improved his house and his fields, never wore a sour face about weather or people, continually smiled on the world, and above all treated his bad bargain with Simon Wilbur as a joke of which he, Duval, was the point.

The old man, pricked in conscience, had actually gone to offer a reduction in the price he had accepted, though in mortal dread of what his wife would say afterward; but Duval insisted that finished business is dead business, and must not be brought to life again.

Moose Creek learned of this, and adding it to the other established virtues of Duval, decided by an almost unanimous vote that the town had acquired an ideal citizen.

Nevertheless, no matter how greatly they appreciated Duval, they could not help being curious about him. And when it was learned that Duval had been in New York before he came West, that he had seen there a beautiful horse at a horse show, that he had now bought that horse and was having it shipped to Moose Creek, was it any wonder that half the town assembled on the morning when the train was due?

When the train arrived, it was almost characteristic of Duval that he was not present and had sent down Simon Wilbur to bring the horse home. When the door was rolled back and the gangplank fixed, the representatives of Moose Creek saw a tall, lean, smooth-shaven man, who looked sixty but might be seventy, issue from the shadows of the car and lead down the plank a most disappointing chestnut mare.

It was true that she picked up her feet daintily going down the plank, but she had a long, ugly head, her withers were high, and her neck was painfully long. So were her legs.

"Duval's been sold!" was the opinion of everyone except Pete, who walked around her with care, lifted her blanket, thumped her shoulders, felt her bone.

The old man who accompanied her—a marvel to Moose Creek that any man should be so extravagant as to ship a horse from New York *and* a man to take care of it—turned to Pete with a smile that appeared crookedly, and only upon one side of his face.

"*You* know a horse, I guess!" said he.

He immediately added that he would like to know the way to Duval's place, and Simon Wilbur at once took charge.

They went up the street, the two old men in the seat of the buckboard and the mare led behind, going at a rather shuffling trot that knocked up the heaped and rutted dust into a cloud. She pulled back lazily at the rope, moreover, and with her lower lip flopping as she went by the grocery store, she looked to Marian Lane like a cartoon of a horse.

"What did he mean?" asked Doc Murphy, of Pete, "what did he mean? As if we that been pretty nigh born on hossback, didn't know a hoss when we seen one?"

Pete grew remote and almost surly.

"Aw, I dunno," said he. "Maybe she can move!"

"Not more'n barely," said Doc. "You seen her go down the street?"

Pete's answer was considered very odd indeed.

"Picture hosses never carried my money!" For Pete had been East, and had bet and lost his one big roll on the ponies.

The name of the mare was considered odd, also. For her old groom had said she was called "Discretion," or "Cherry," for short.

In the meantime, the buckboard jogged up the hill and Simon Wilbur tried his expert hand on the new arrival. The latter was perfectly willing to talk about himself, and how many years he had been a groom and in what stables, but on the important point, which was Duval, he knew nothing. He never had heard the name before. He never had seen the man. He did not know whether Duval was young or old! All he knew was that he had been hired to take the mare all the way West.

"Is she worth it all?" asked Simon rather spitefully.

"Well," said the groom, considering, "she can jump enough to make her hind legs follow her forelegs."

At last they reached the old sagging wooden gate through which one entered the Duval place, and here Wilbur drew up.

"You'll be goin' back soon, I reckon?"

"I dunno," said the groom, who had said that his name was Henry. "Might be that he'd like to have me handle the mare for a few days and get her on her feed."

So he waved good-bye to Wilbur and advanced through the gate, leading the mare.

Simon took the trouble, however, to call out: "Hey, Duval! Here she is!"

His call was answered almost at once by a shrill whistle. And glancing back through a gap among the trees that grew thick at the margin of the property, he had an unexpected sight of the lifeless mare jerking away from Henry the groom and running across the meadows toward the house. She went with her head stretched out and with a long, bounding gallop so different from the gait of a cow pony that Wilbur laughed as he watched it. This singular stride faded her out of view almost at once, and Wilbur jogged on down the road still chuckling to himself.

The manner in which the mare had responded to the whistle had not surprised Henry the groom, however. As he strolled on toward the cabin, which seemed to him a greater novelty than all else, he stared at this and the sheds behind it as if they were so many human faces, each worthy of separate consideration, each expressing something worth adding to his total. So he rounded the corner of the house and came in view of Duval.

The latter was engaged in walking around and around the chestnut mare, a task which she made difficult, for though she dropped her head to pick at the grass now and then, she insisted on following her owner closely with ears that pricked with pleasure.

"Cherry hasn't changed a bit," said Duval, his back to the groom. "She give you plenty of trouble on the way out, I reckon, stranger?"

"Oh," said Henry, "she's got a mind of her own, but I like folks that can think for themselves."

Now, at the sound of his voice, Duval stiffened a little, like one who hears something in the distance and fixes his attention upon it.

At last he said curtly: "Put her in the pasture corral over there by that shed."

"Certainly, sir," said Henry, and taking up the lead rope, he took the mare toward the corral.

Leaving it there, he went with his usual lack of haste up the path to the house. Just inside the shack he paused again, not to look at the owner, but to survey the furnishings as though they told him more about Duval than the face of the man could do.

The latter, in the meantime, sat at ease in his most comfortable chair, with his hands interlocked and his gray eyes quietly studying the groom.

"Henry?" he said at last.

Henry straightened himself.

"Yes, sir," said he.

"A long trip, wasn't it?"

"A very long trip," agreed Henry.

"And after such a long trip," went on Duval in his gentle way, "in order to make it worth while, Henry, what do you want?"

At this, Henry no longer smiled his secret smile, but laughter rose up and shook him with a dry passion of mirth.

"Why, sir," he said, "I ain't hardly had a chance to look around and see what's worth taking!"

This last speech, in spite of its oddity, Duval accepted with a nod.

"Sit down, Henry," he said kindly.

"Thank you, sir; I'll stand," said Henry.

"You have plans of returning at once, I suppose?"

"Me, sir? Not at all, sir! I was raised in the country; that's where I learned horses."

"Now I remember, of course. You've always said that horsemen have to grow up on the grass. But do you mean that you like it out here? Hardly that, Henry!"

"Why not, sir? Old men go back to the soil, sir."

"But these big open spaces are only meant for people who have been born in them. Strangers never can quite adapt themselves to the range, Henry."

"No, sir?"

"No, as a matter of fact, they find the elevation a great trial. They're apt to grow short of breath. They're even apt to grow dizzy and fall from a cliff!"

"Me," said Henry genially, "I always been used to heights, sir."

"Ah, yes?" said Duval.

"Besides," said Henry, "I've got to be an old

man, sir, and so I've left all of my affairs in pretty good order!"

"You're a wise man," said Duval.

"Left letters," said Henry, "to be opened a month after I left New York, unless the bank heard from me before. Letters about my will, and such things, sir. So it would be pretty hard to see how trouble would bother me, sir!"

"Of course!" said Duval. "You really should sit down, Henry. Out here, one doesn't stand on formalities."

"Just as you please, sir," said Henry, and sank into a chair.

"You think of staying on, then?"

"I don't mind if I do. As I was saying, I take to the open air, and it takes to me. You'd have room for me here, sir?"

"You can see for yourself that it's a small house."

"Well, I wouldn't want to crowd you, Mr.—"

"Certainly not!" said Duval hastily. "I was only considering your own comfort, Henry."

"Ah, sir," said Henry. "That was always your kind way, sir."

"Besides, in this part of the country, we don't 'sir' one another."

"Very good, sir. I'll remember that."

"If you insist on staying?"

"Insist? Of course I don't want to press in on you, Mr.—"

"No pressing in, Henry. Delighted to have you, of course. You have a bag with you?"

"Yes. Wilbur brought it up in his rig. I left it at the gate when I brought up Cherry."

"Henry, I'm a curious man and want to ask you a question."

"Thank you!"

"What brought you out with Cherry?"

"That makes a story," said he.

"I'd like to hear it, if I'm not prying."

"Well, then, when the news came of your drowning—which was a shock to me, Mr.—"

"No doubt it was," cut in Duval. "Go on."

"I remembered that you could swim only about twice as well as an otter. It was a half-mile pull to the shore from where that boat upset—"

"No, nearly a mile."

"All right, sir, but I looked at the place and all at once I was sure that you could have made the land. Why didn't you, then? Because you didn't want to! Why didn't you want to? What would make you want to go off-stage? Nothing, maybe, except a few debts! And it wasn't your style to scratch at the last minute."

"You're full of compliments," said Duval. "But I'm still interested."

"Besides, the boat looked too small to beat you. I don't know how to put it any other way!"

"Thank you," said Duval. "Go on, Henry."

"When your things went at auction, I was on hand, and I saw Slater and Grimm bid on the mare. Now, no matter what happened to the rest of the stable, and the house, and the furniture, and all that, I made up my mind that even if you were dead, you'd stir in your grave when Discretion was sold!

"I sat up there in the stand at the auction and watched them prance her up and down—they had a fool of a boy that couldn't show a whit. In fact, she never had right hands on her except yours, sir!

"The bidding went to three thousand. But Slater and Grimm wouldn't let her go, of course, at the price. They entered her afterward in the Chester Point-to-Point and gave young Enderley the mount.

"I used to drop in at the stables of Slater and Grimm nearly every day and have a look at her and a talk with the boys. Then one day they told me that she was sold. A man from the West had seen her shown last winter, liked her, and now he bid up for her—bid high enough to make even Slater smile! They were shipping her out.

"Now, sir, I put two and two together and thought that it made a thousand! So I said I'd always wanted to take a trip West, and I'd go along with her, for the chance to travel, and no pay! Of course they took me, and that's how I'm here.

"I knew, somehow, that if you were living you were Duval. And so it turned out!"

"So it turned out," agreed Duval without enthusiasm.

He stood up suddenly.

"Bring up your suitcase, Henry."

"Thank you," said he, and went at once to fetch it.

Henry, soon was coming up the path leaning far over against the weight of his suitcase, his mouth compressed with effort. Duval hurried down to him and took the burden lightly in his hand.

"Whew!" gasped Henry, relieved. "I'm turning into an older man than I thought, sir."

Reaching the house Duval laid the suitcase on the bunk in the corner of the room.

"Unlock it, Henry," said he.

Henry looked askance at him, hesitated, but then obeyed. He stood anxiously by.

"I'm going through it," said Duval.

"Sir?" said Henry. "Going through it!"

"Yes, stand away from me."

All inside was packed very neatly, and with great care Duval lifted out article by article, until the case was half emptied.

Through the rest of it he passed his hands, feeling here and there until he touched something that seemed to tell him what he wanted to know, for he looked at Henry with the slightest of smiles.

"I thought so," said Duval, and drew from the suitcase a package wrapped in oiled silk, beneath which the texture of chamois showed through.

Fingering this, a faint gritting of metal on metal was heard.

"I'll take this," said Duval.

Henry was biting his lip.

"I don't know—" began he.

"You don't understand, Henry" said Duval. "I lead a quiet life here, as you can see for yourself. When you realize that, Henry, I'm afraid that you won't find yourself as much at home here as you expected to be. Am I right?"

Henry sighed, but then shrugged his high, narrow shoulders.

"Blood lines and performance is what I bet on," said he. "I'll stay here with you, sir!"

"Very well, then. Your bunk is that one in the other corner. Take your stuff over there. You'll find some shelves behind that curtain. Get into old clothes; everyone works in Moose Creek, Henry."

Saying this, he turned his back on Henry and descended through a trap in the floor down a ladder into the cellar. There he dug a small hole in a corner next to the wall, placed the package in its wrapping of oiled silk in the aperture, and then covered it over and tramped down the moist earth. The remnant of loose soil he scattered here and there, before returning to the floor above.

7

Woman, like the elephant, never forgets and cannot forgive; so it was that Marian Lane behind her emotionless smile was filled with bitterness when she remembered how Duval in their last encounter had checked, thwarted, and scorned her by his superior strength.

He had given an acid flavor to her old passion for discovering who Duval might be; she transferred a portion of her curiosity, naturally, to the very plain-looking chestnut mare which had arrived for him from the East, and promptly she decided that the secret virtues of that animal—since it was not to be expected that Duval would waste money and time on a thing no better than she looked to be—must be investigated.

She hit at once on a plan for making the investigation, and started to work on Charlie Nash the next time he entered the store.

"Poor Charlie," she said. "I suppose that you're terribly embarrassed now?"

"About what?" he asked her.

"Why, the way everyone is laughing at your friend."

"You mean Duval, of course?" said Charlie

Nash. "Nobody's laughing at Duval in this here town, honey. Unless it's you. And what's your call?"

"At Duval, and his mare," she insisted. "When I saw the poor, pitiful thing going up the street, I couldn't believe my eyes."

"Look here, Marian," he objected. "She's got points. She's got bone—"

"She's full of bones!" said the girl.

"And legs, too."

"Yards of em," said she. "If the mare's any good, Charlie, what is it good for?"

"You can't go on a man's looks," said Charlie stubbornly, "or on a hoss's, either."

"But *what* is she good for?"

"How can I tell?"

"Does she *look* good for anything?"

"As I was sayin'—"

"Stuff!" said she. "He simply doesn't know horses, and you have to admit it!"

On that range, this was far worse than saying that a man could neither read nor write.

"I'll bet she can run," said Charlie, desperate.

"How much will you bet?"

"Anything you want."

"I'll give you odds," she answered. "Two dollars to one."

"Who'd be the judge?"

"Why, there's the race at the end of the rodeo at Kendry tomorrow."

"You know Duval. He won't—"

"I don't know him at all."

"You know he won't leave the farm."

"He'll do anything for a friend, you always say."

"Well, and it's true. Everybody knows that."

"You're his friend, I suppose?"

"I reckon I am!"

"Then why don't you ask him?"

"Maybe I will. But he won't enter Cherry."

"Not for a friend?"

"Well, if I have a chance to see him—"

"I saw him go into Pete's just this minute."

He was cornered, and sullenly swinging around, he crossed to Pete's Place and found Duval there treating his new companion, Henry, to a tall glass of beer.

"Partner," said Charlie, "will you do something for me?"

"Anything I can," answered Duval, offhand.

"Try that mare of yours in the race at Kendry tomorrow. I've bet that she could run!"

He saw the face of Duval darken, and added hastily: "I ain't bet she'd win. I know she couldn't beat Dave Shine's blood hoss. But I'd bet she can move a little."

Duval flushed a trifle.

"I'd a pile rather not," said he. "Unless you keep me to that promise."

"I'm gunna keep you!" said Nash. "Doggone it, man, I don't want to bother you, but you'd enjoy the rodeo, anyway! Will you come?"

"I've given you a promise," said Duval shortly. "I suppose I'll be there!"

And he was!

When the riders lined up for the race, while loud voices were shouting bets and offering odds, Duval appeared on Discretion in the starting row.

There were already eight known horses in the string, and not one but made Discretion look a sad thing indeed, especially when she grew excited and began to prance, throwing her long legs about.

Charlie Nash, grimly bent on supporting a friend whom he had introduced to trouble, savagely bet a borrowed hundred dollars, and got odds of eight to one—high odds for such a race as this. Then he returned to the place where Marian Lane stood near the finish with a big black camera box in her hands. She was setting up a tripod as he came near.

"It ain't gunna be such a close finish as all that," said Charlie gloomily. "They won't need a picture to show which one got first. When Dave Shine's blood hoss gets warmed up, he's gunna swaller this whole field."

He added, grimly: "Then you'll feel a lot better!"

"Why," she said sweetly, "it's no disgrace if poor Duval doesn't know horses. I'm sure he's shown that he knows a great many other things."

"You got a mean way about you sometimes, Marian," the boy assured her. "What's Duval ever done to you?"

"Hush!" said she. "They're about to start—and —oh, he's left at the post. They ought to call them back and start over—what a shame! Will he pull up? Will he pull up, Charlie?"

She asked it eagerly as the starter's gun exploded while Discretion was turned broadside to the course. The rest swept away in a thundering line, while Discretion, floundering behind, slowly straightened and then began to labor after the field.

Her efforts brought great laughter from the spectators.

"And *that's* Mr. Duval's fine horse!" said the girl scornfully. "He *ought* to pull her up, even if he doesn't!"

However, Duval was not pulling her up; he made

no effort to overtake the others, but simply handrode the chestnut mare. So the runners swung around the first half of the circle, to the point where the early leaders began to tire and now a fine black stallion rushed out from the pack as though they were standing still.

A wild yell of triumph went up for that favorite.

"There goes Duster! There goes Shine's hoss. The race is over, boys!"

The race seemed indeed over, as the last bend was rounded, when through the tiring pack cut a chestnut streak that seemed to make but one stride to two of the others. Duval, and Discretion, coming like the wind—so uncomfortably fast that all shouting ceased, and Charlie Nash, standing on the fence, raised both his hands, whispering: "Eight to one. Oh, you ugly beauty! Come on, Cherry!"

Cherry came on, but not fast enough. Those who watched wondered why Duval had not taken up his whip. Even handridden, she was making a race of it and gaining on Duster's frightened rider, but what if a whip were laid on her? Indeed, it looked as though her head were drawn in by the pull which Duval was giving her!

The rest of the crowd gave tongue like a hungry pack—and as they yelled, the right rein of Cherry's bridle parted. They saw Duval sway back; they saw the mare dart ahead.

It was like the release of a stone from the hand of the thrower. With every leap she gained momentum. Her long neck was stretched straight out, her ugly, lean head was snaky as she thrust forward, and the very wind of her going seemed to have flattened her ears along her neck.

She looked no longer awkward. She was like a

thing with wings, and every stroke carried her swiftly up toward the stallion.

He would have won, however, if the rider had done his duty. But just before the wire, looking back in fear at that sound of hoofs, the youngster let the stallion swerve.

That was fatal. Discretion shot under the wire first by a head.

That, however, was not the important thing in the eyes of the winning rider, for as Duval looked to the side of the track in crossing the line, he saw the big black square of the camera aimed not at Discretion at all, but at the height of his own head!

He jerked his face in the other direction, but somehow he knew that he was too late.

Already she knew too much, he guessed, and now she was well on the way to learning everything!

Back at the start, the girl was gripping Charlie's arm. His was almost the only voice to celebrate. He and Pete the bartender, who strangely enough had chosen to bet on the mare of his own free will and not out of loyalty to Cherry's rider.

"Listen to me, Charlie! Collect your bets tomorrow. I have to go home. I have to go fast! Do you hear me, Charlie?"

"Sure I hear you! Can she run, Marian? Can she run?"

"Like the wind—she's wonderful—only get me away quickly, quickly!"

"Sure," said Charlie, sobered. "But what's the matter?"

"I forgot something at the store. Oh, make the horses fly on the way back!"

8

It was night before Charlie Nash's sweating horses brought the girl back to Moose Creek.

"They's something wrong, Marian," said he. "You're sick, or something!"

She laughed, and tried to make that laughter sound natural, but knew that she had failed.

"Maybe I'm *about* to be ill, but I'm not now," she told him. "You go along home, Charlie. There's nothing for you to worry about and nothing that you can help me in. Good night. I'm glad you made a big winning *plus* my dollar!"

She was gone into the darkness of the store before he could answer, and then he heard the front door locked and double-locked.

She had no faith in the locked front door, though she did have some in the chain and bolt which she fastened across it. The windows she locked also, and despaired of securing them in a better manner.

Then, lamp in hand, she walked back down the aisle, while the shadows rose and fell softly around her with every step she made. The rear windows she secured in the same manner.

The cellar door, also, possessed a bolt, though it

seemed to her now a most feeble one. She shot it home and after that she had to pass through the door that led to the rear stairs, lock this behind her without the additional security of any bolt, and climb up to her own chamber.

The door stood wide open and for a moment she dreaded to enter, leaning sick and helpless against the jamb, for it seemed that even if the rest of the building had been empty, here she would certainly find what she feared.

But when she raised the lamp above her head, it showed her nothing but emptiness.

She set her teeth, entered with a quick step, and closed and locked this last door of all.

There remained one last barrier which she could erect against the world, and that was the open window, which she closed and fastened with the ridiculously weak catch that was supposed to keep it from being opened from without!

That done, she fell to work. Adjoining her room was a small closet which she used as a dark cabinet. No one else in the town developed films and she derived a vitally necessary little income from this work. Rapidly she prepared the acid bath, immersed the film from her own camera, and then waited desperately until the proper time had elapsed.

She forgot the small, pulsing sounds that continually seemed to steal up the stairs and stand listening outside her door. At last she could take the film from the bath and hold it to a light.

Her heart leaped in fierce triumph, for it was Duval's face she had snapped. Clearly, unblurred by all the speed of the horse, it stood before her, and she faced around at her door in victorious defiance.

There was still the printing to be managed. It was long into the night before it was accomplished. She struck off three copies, and having made them, she sat down to write:

Dear Eleanor,

This is a hasty note, first to apologize for not writing for so long and most of all to send you this snapshot. A strange fellow has come to Moose Creek and made a great place for himself here. You can see even from the picture, I think, that he's not a type, and in the flesh he's a great deal more remarkable. He has a pale face and gray eyes. That's not much of a description, but if you've ever seen the man, it will mean a great deal to you. The reason I'm sending the picture, dear, is that I want to have him identified if I can. I don't want talk made, but if you could quietly show this picture to a few people you know, I'd be glad to hear if they know him. I have reasons for thinking that he's quite a horseman, and among your Long Island or Maryland friends who hunt and follow the races, there may very well be someone who will recognize him.

You might say that this is a picture of the typical cowpuncher, who recently won a race in a rodeo at Kendry, in the Far West.

The real point is that I don't think that he's typical at all. I intend to write to you again soon, and make it a real letter.

She hesitated for something else to say, then signed the letter, placed it with a print of the picture in the envelope, and sealed it and stamped it.

Then she sat down to wait for the morning.

Of all the hours of her life there was none that

compared with the strain of that long waiting. Listening with aching nerves, a dozen times she knew she heard the faint metallic rattle of the front door of the store opening, heard the unlocking of the door at the foot of her stairs, and then again the pause of someone outside her very room. Once she could have sworn that she saw the knob slowly turning, and gasping with horror, she picked up a small bulldog revolver and levelled it with both hands.

Nothing happened!

So she wrapped herself in her bathrobe and lay down on the bed to rest with a book—and with the gun! There was no rest. The print swam into a confusion of shadows, and every moment her haunted eyes were lifted toward the door, or toward the window.

It was like a blessing to her when she saw the gray of the dawn begin, but never had it lingered so slowly, never had she so prayed for the honest sun.

At last it came; the rose died from the sky, the brilliant golden light was everywhere, and springing up from the bed she prepared to go down at once to the street.

With nervous hands she prepared her hair, put a hat over it, rubbed color into her cheeks, and then with much concern looked at the shadows beneath her eyes.

Never had she wanted anything as she wanted coffee now.

First, she had to dispose of the two extra prints and the film itself, and these she placed for the time being in the book which she had attempted to read that night, a much battered old copy of *Lorna Doone* which she had taken because she felt it might give her ease from its very familiarity.

She was ready now. First she listened at the door. Then she boldly unbolted, unlocked it, and flung it wide.

She held herself very well until she was halfway up the aisle of the store, and then she went to pieces and fled to the big front door.

It was so early that not a chimney in Moose Creek was smoking as she hurried up the street, and every step gave her additional confidence, additional courage, until in half a block the terrors of the night seemed more fatiguing than real.

She could almost have laughed at them by the time she reached the post office, but when she held the letter at the slot in the wall, she hesitated again.

She turned away. She half crumpled the letter in her hand as she did so. Then the last impulse won, for she stepped back and with a decisive flick shot the envelope away—away into the hands of the law, which would cherish it, protect it, waste blood of brave men for its sake, if necessary. In that instant she felt a warm assurance that she had gained a mighty ally and started wheels too huge for even Duval to stop!

Then lassitude overcame Marian Lane.

She went dreamily back down the sidewalk, the loose boards creaking a bit beneath her step, and smiled vaguely at the open door of the store, remembering the horror with which she had flung it open only a few moments before.

She closed it again, yawned at the blank street, and returned slowly upstairs for a cold plunge, then to breakfast quickly and so to work before any early orders might come in, as they often did.

But life seemed a little blank and dreary to

Marian Lane as she opened the door of her room and went in to prepare for the day, after such a night as this. She was unnerved, too, by an increasing pity for Duval, who had done no wrong, at least in Moose Creek. Here he was a hero, a champion of might, a tower of strength, a defender of the weak.

But she had hoped to take the hero in the palm of her hand and make him tremble.

Now that her mind was more clear, she wished suddenly to see how good a likeness she actually had taken, and so opened *Lorna Doone,* to find that the pictures and the film were gone!

It was so impossible that she laughed.

She told herself that she had really put them in some other place, and was opening the drawer of her writing table when she saw the letter that was placed on top of it.

It was written—or rather printed—in very dim ink that made hardly a mark on the surface. As a matter of fact, it seemed to have been done with a brush that possessed an extremely fine point, for some of the letters blurred one into another.

She read:

Dear Marian,
 As I watched you through the window last night and this morning you sure made a mighty pretty picture. . . .

She ran to the window and jerked it open. The sill projected well to either side and to the right it seemed to her that the dusty paint had been cleaned a little. On the rusted pipe that drained away the roof-water, she told herself that there was

STRANGE COURAGE

a distinctly brighter place where a hand might have grasped it for support.

But how could anyone have climbed here from the outside?

She leaned out and stared down toward the ground. It still seemed impossible. There was a sheer drop of twenty feet. There was no possible way of mounting except by the slight indentations between the boards and the drainage pipe itself. Even a sailor would hardly have liked the task of making that climb.

But then to sit there in the cold wind through hours, as it seemed, of the night and the morning. To remain there, certainly, until he had seen her putting the pictures in the book! That was broad day, and a dozen windows of neighboring houses gaped at him, yet he had remained there until she left the room! Then entered—then swiftly slipped down the pipe to the ground, leaving no trace behind him except that the window was unlatched!

She ran back to the letter, which seemed now even dimmer than before, and read it again.

> As I watched you through the window last night and this morning you sure made a pretty picture. I was powerful tempted to knock on the window and tell you so!

He could have dropped his slang, she thought bitterly, if he had known that she had seen the titles of his books.

> That was a pretty clear picture that you made of me, and I didn't think that you'd mind if I borrowed them.

But here I been looking into the book and wondering a pile if you ever read it before because the girl in there is sure a winner. She don't seem to be full of nothing but trust and I'd lay my money that she made men better. . . .

It was certainly true that the writing was now so extraordinarily dim that she could hardly make it out.

But with straining eyes she found her place again and struggled on.

. . .and never made a poor cowpuncher burglarize snapshots out of a girl's room and then go and rob the Federal mail which is what I have to hurry and go do before the folks get up. But in the windup I got to say again that you made a mighty pretty picture lying on the bed and pointing that gun at the door which maybe you didn't notice that the caps was all pulled?

Respectfully yours,
Duval.

She could make out the last words only by using a bit of imagination. But now she hurried to the little revolver and opened it. It was quite true. Every cap had been removed from the cartridges, and she might have pulled the trigger as often as she pleased without firing a shot!

It changed her picture of Duval suddenly and completely. He had returned from the rodeo faster even than Charlie Nash's sweating horses. He had entered the store, he had been to her room, he had found the weapon and made it harmless. Then he had slipped out from the building.

Why had he done this, then, rather than encounter her suddenly in the dark and take the camera from her with all its evidence which he so much feared?

She thought, with a start, of hurrying to the post office to give warning of what might be attempted, but she saw at once that this was impossible. Totally impossible, and all that had happened on this night, together with Duval's confession, could never be mentioned to any other human being in the world.

He, with a cunning insight, had known it, and taken that advantage to leave the letter behind him.

She picked it up again, but to her amazement, she found that there was hardly a trace of anything upon the smooth paper, and that trace, real or imagined, now vanished under her very eyes.

How he had mixed that mysterious ink, she could not guess, but she told herself that Duval had a thousand accomplishments which must be behind locked doors from any investigation of hers. At least, there was one secret which they shared in common, and she laughed a little grimly as she thought of it.

9

In the dusk of the day Duval came from the horse shed where the mule and the saddle horse had been duly stalled and fed, to find the steam of great cookery ascending from the stove, and old Henry perspiring before it.

"Too much food for tonight, Henry," he explained. "There's work for me to do and I can't overeat."

"Night work?" asked Henry, his eyes gleaming under their white brows. "*I* could tell you about some night work that's been haunting me all the afternoon."

"You can? You always were a prowling old cat that woke up at sunset. What is it now, Henry?"

Henry extended a long-handled granite cooking spoon.

"Yonder, over the hills—" He choked with a sudden emotion.

"You look as if you were going to cry, Henry. Who do you want to do now?"

"Thousands and thousands," murmured Henry, "and a safe that would fall down like a house of cards if you blew at it. If you touched it, it would open its door to shake hands. It's a fine safe, a good safe, an honest safe, it's a safe that makes friends!"

"Business is as business does," said Duval. "You old scoundrel, where have you been?"

"I been over the hills and far away," said Henry. "I might of known you wouldn't talk to me about it. Two weeks' pay and a lot of extras for about eleven hundred men—two weeks' pay and a lot of extras, I tell you. Do you hear me?"

"Oh, I hear you clearly enough. You want to take more scalps, Henry? I should think that you'd be willing to retire, by this time, and rest on your laurels."

"Stay here with you!" said Henry slowly. "Ay, and maybe I would. Maybe I would chuck the other thing and stay here with you, but how long'll you be here?"

"I? Why, forever, of course. Isn't this my home, Henry?"

"Your home," said Henry gloomily, "is somewhere between the Rue de la Paix and hell, and right well you know it!"

"Tush," said Duval. "That street is too short and the other one is too warm, and I much prefer it here, Henry."

"You'll be off," remarked Henry. "Stay here, I think I could! This'd be a place to live and die in. Seein' things grow up out of the earth and die back into it, I mean, till the growing and the dying of men don't matter so much. But—you won't stay long. You'll be flying as fast as steam'll take you. Only if you'd listen to me, I could tell you of a way to spend a night that would be worth something to both of us!"

"Could you?"

"I'm sayin' so!"

"Henry, there's nothing in the world that really interests you except the elbows and the dicks."

"Me?" said Henry, amazed.

"You! You can't get along without 'em."

"Without that mangy lot?"

"Of course you can't, and you'll know it, if you think for a moment. What would you have for spice in life, Henry, if half a dozen detectives weren't nosing about the country for you all the time?"

"They'll never get me again," said Henry solemnly. "Never again!"

"How old are you, Henry?"

"Rising fifty," said Henry without blushing.

"Rising it so far it's out of reach and sight," said his companion. "How many years have you spent in jail?"

"Oh, a few stretches. Maybe twenty."

"Twenty years in jail, and you'll be ten more, if you live that long!"

"No," said Henry, as gravely as before. "I keep a gun now not for the other guy but for myself! The next time they grab at me, they'll catch nothing but air. I don't figure on dying in the stripes."

The manner in which he spoke made Duval, it appeared, put off his casual and caustic speech.

"What's your scheme tonight, or some other night?" he asked.

"For this night, and no other," said Henry. "I've been over to the Broom and Carson Company the other day. I've seen their office. Why, any fool could walk into it, and once inside, there's the safe that fills the whole end of a room. I tell you, it's mine and yours, if you'll come with me, and if you won't, I'll go by myself!"

"Will you?" asked Duval.

"I will! One taste of soap and soup would knock the whole face off it. There's a couple of hundred grand inside it or I'm a fool and a liar!"

"What would you do with it, old fellow?" asked Duval.

"What would I do with it? I'd find a way to use it. I might buy a farm beside yours, and settle down here."

Duval smiled.

"They'd have you in two days, probably."

"The dicks? Nobody knows me in this neck of the woods, and that's one thing that put the idea into my head, I tell you! I'll have it as easy as walk! I'll bring it back—"

"Not here, Henry."

"Not here?"

"No. If you go for it, then keep away from me."

"I'd be missed and suspected, then."

"It's true," muttered Duval. "You infernal old troublemaker, keep quietly at home. If you want money, you have a gun at my head. How much will you take?"

"Money?" said Henry. "Money?"

He laughed softly.

"It ain't the money! You know that. It's the feel of the game."

Duval sighed. "I'm going to make you change your mind," he declared.

"Change it? I can't change it. Dying wouldn't hardly change me that way!"

"Kinkaid would, though, from what I hear of him."

"Kinkaid? I never heard of him."

"Neither did I, except in the distance. He's a man-catcher, Henry, who works for the fun of the game, just as you work for fun at the other end of it. He's gone three years on nothing but one trial, they tell me! I've been hearing about him for two weeks, off and on. Tonight I'm going out to meet him."

"Going to meet him!" exclaimed Henry. "Are you crazy?"

"I'd be crazy not to. He's to be at the dance tonight. He's likely to hear something about me there. Well, I don't want that. I don't want him to get suspicions of his own and—"

"What if he knows you?"

"If he knows me?"

Duval shrugged his shoulders.

He had been undressing as he talked, and now was preparing to step into a galvanized tub into which he had poured his bucket of water and a hot kettleful from the stove.

"If he knows me, that's guns, Henry. But he's all Western. He's lived here, worked here, grown famous here; and that's why we don't hear more of him in New York, and other places. But I want to walk under his eyes, be introduced to him, shake hands with him. Then he's not likely to think I'm dangerous and worth a little study."

Henry nodded, with open admiration in his eyes.

"If I had what you got," said he, "I'd have the world! I'd have the crown jewels of England out of the Tower and take 'em away in a grip at noonday. Why, there ain't a thing you couldn't have, fixed the way you are!"

"Then why don't I have it, Henry?"

"Because," said the other, "you're too good to

be bad, and too bad to be good! That's the straight of it! Hurry up. I'll lay out your dark suit. Are you going to slick up?"

"About halfway. That's all."

"And you're going to the dance, too? You really mean it?"

"I mean it, and *you* are going to stay home!"

He paused in soaping his body to level a forefinger like a gun at Henry, and the latter grinned with enjoyment.

"Sure," said he. "I'll be home. I'll be here when you come back!"

But his keen eye flickered away from that of Duval.

10

It was a big dance, a dressed-up dance.

Spurred boots and bandannas and rough shirts remained in bunkhouses and from the pegs on the walls wrinkled, unfitted suits of blue serge were taken down, brushed with a fond hope that the spots of yesteryear might not show their faces, and sorrowed over because old sins would not be hidden. They washed in tubs of cold water, those men of the range, and scrubbed themselves with laundry soap and rubbed themselves dry with harsh cotton towels. They dressed with care. They donned fancifully colored shirts; they buckled chokingly high turn-over collars around their bulky necks and then stood before dim little cracked mirrors, tiptoe with agonized effort while they tied white neckties, with little streaks of colored flowers down the center.

They brushed their hair and cursed and watered the tangles which insisted on standing upright in spite of patient labor. Their faces were red with shaving and with work when at last they squeezed their feet into old shoes, and blacked the dingy toes of them, letting the heels take care of themselves.

After that, miserable, pinched in many places,

they passed one another in review. They told each other that they looked "fine," that they "certainly looked fit," and that they would stop the show when they began to prance. Then they climbed into carts, into buckboards, and drove from five to thirty miles to attend the festivities.

They found an orchestra tired but enduring, supported by certain quantities of whisky and unlimited applause. They found a big barn floor polished with wax ground in by a bale of hay drawn across it by volunteers earlier in the day. There were bunting streamers stretched across the rafters, Japanese lanterns burning dimly, low down, lamps bracketed against the walls, and a thin haze of cigarette smoke that seemed to grow thicker as it mounted toward the shadows of the loft. They found a gay crowd, moreover, that made up for the shaky music, the dimness of the lights. For those who had worked so hard to get here refused resolutely to have a bad time. They found, moreover, at this dance, a king of the ball, named Richard Kinkaid, and a queen also, who was Marian Lane as a matter of course.

"Dick Kinkaid's taken a tumble at last!"

"Watch him and Marian Lane! Look at his grin. He ain't smiled for seven years, they say; looks like his face'll crack, tonight!"

The great Kinkaid at last showed one touching human strain!

He was an Ajax of the mountain, lofty, nobly made. He was no boy, but well over thirty, and with a dozen years of big achievements behind him. He was one of those who, it seems, are forever on the frontier of the world, loving trouble for its own poisonous sake and hunting danger as lovers hunt for their beloved.

There are ever two classes of these men—those who carelessly defy the law and make their own rules of living; and there are those more cautious spirits, though equally grim, who exercise their strength in defense of the law. But both classes have at heart the same overmastering passion—the desire for combat.

Richard Kinkaid was of the second class, but all men, whether good or evil doers, found it equally hard to look into that dark, stern face; for his eye was always quick, and with or without his will, it was forever looking for only one thing—offense!

It was hardly a wonder that women had meant nothing to Richard Kinkaid. His life was lived among men, his battles were of course with them, and where his fights were, there was his heart also!

Tonight, however, the unexpected blow had fallen, and he, looking down at Marian Lane, as many another man had looked, suddenly began to wonder if that delicate and dolllike face could be lighted by any real emotion, and if those wide, childish eyes could begin to have a woman's meaning.

The frown that made the crease between his eyes relaxed. And Kinkaid began to smile for she, also, was smiling up at him, speaking very little, but listening, listening, and seeming to drink deep of all he said.

He danced a little, stiffly, clumsily. Then, several times, he sat out with her and told her why he had come to this place—because even if his coming were known, certain men for whom he was looking might perhaps appear here, drawn by the irresistible lure of pleasure and hoping that he would forget.

He laughed a little as he said this, and the ring of

iron was in his voice again, as when he spoke of his wars.

It was late in the evening. Rather, it was early morning, when the next interruption came with the entry of a new excitement. It sent a buzz around the hall, and the murmur came even to the ears of big Richard Kinkaid, as he stood talking with Colonel Hope, old, gentle, chivalrous, famous from the Indian wars.

"What are they all talking about?" asked Kinkaid. "Who are they looking at?"

He himself had been occupying the forefront of attention up to this moment, but it never occurred to Kinkaid that he was jealous of such notoriety. He would have said that he was above such a thing! However, it is undoubtedly true that from the very first instant he felt a pinching of his heart as the Colonel answered: "By my stars, I didn't expect to see him here! This is a greater surprise than your coming, even. Because you've showed yourself at these places before, Kinkaid. But unless I'm seeing dreams that young fellow yonder—that one who has just come in—d'you see him!"

"No," said Kinkaid untruly.

"Look again. You can't mistake him. Rather tall—not huge like you. But tall, with a pale face. That's the man of Moose Creek!"

"Are they raising men in Moose Creek, these days?" asked Kinkaid, with his usual half-suppressed sneer.

The Colonel did not appear to understand that slur. He went on enthusiastically: "By the Lord, that fellow has the real steel in him. He's the one who took young Charlie Nash—good lad but wild—and took his gun away from him—dodged bullets to do it, mind you!—confoundedly heroic! Took his gun away, laid him out, took him home and sobered him up—made his peace with the sheriff—made Charlie his fast friend for life! Confoundedly fine, I call that. A fellw in ten million. Why, Kinkaid, they love that lad in Moose Creek. I don't blame them! I wish we had him in *our* section of the country!"

Kinkaid, in fact, had noted this newcomer the first instant he entered the room; he followed him now as he passed across the floor. A dance began, a tag dance; the man of Moose Creek was dancing, his lady remaining safely in his arms, untouched by any hand.

"What's his name?"

"Duval."

"I never heard of him before," said Kinkaid bluntly.

"Then you've been out of touch with this section for a good many weeks," said the Colonel with equal frankness. "We've been talking about nothing else. Graceful couple, aren't they?"

Kinkaid looked at the girl, and his heart leaped amazingly, and then fell like a stone.

For it was Marian Lane in the arms of Duval, and truly they made a graceful couple.

They came closer. As she had looked up into the face of big Kinkaid, so now he vowed she was looking up to Duval, except that now she talked, and the man listened, and laughed frankly with her, and seemed at ease beyond imagining.

Kinkaid would have been far more interested if he could have heard their conversation, for Marian Lane was saying: "And the letter was delightful, except—you need not have written slang, I saw your books in your house."

"Then there's one more weight off my mind, and soon we can talk freely. As friends, even?"

"How long were you waiting there outside the window?"

"Not long. I merely went up for a glance."

"But suppose that I'd gone down in the dark and mailed the letter?"

"Poor Eleanor would never have had it. I was waiting in the lower store."

"How did you get in?"

"I can't confess. I may have to come again. But I knew you wouldn't go out."

"Did you?"

"Yes, certainly."

"Why?"

"You were afraid. I saw from the size of your eyes that you were frightened of the man outside your door."

"As if there was one there!"

"There was, for a time."

She shuddered in his arms.

"Yes," he explained. "I thought you deserved a little suffering. So I came up the stairs at one time and stood for a while, breathing rather hard from the climb. That was early in the evening when I suspected that you might really go out as soon as you'd written the letter."

She drew a quick, deep breath.

"You didn't want me to go then?"

"I should have had to meet you in the dark. I didn't want to frighten you as badly as that. Simply give you waking nightmares for a little while."

"Why couldn't you have robbed the post office, as you did later on?"

"Because the postmistress was up playing cards

with a crony. I'd made sure of that, before."

"But when the day came—"

"Yes, then I climbed up again and looked in, in time to see you confide the secret to *Lorna Doone*. Poor Lorna. She never would have approved of such an evening, do you think?"

"Even Lorna would have wanted to know who Duval is!"

"A poor farmer who works hard!"

"But he's something else."

"Nothing that ever has harmed you."

"Who *is* Duval?"

"Have you made a fight out of it? Will you never give in?" he asked her.

"I don't think that I can. I want to know!"

"Suppose that I start prying into Marian Lane?"

"Oh, I'm open as the day. The whole range knows everything about me."

"About beautiful Marian Lane, hard-working Marian Lane, gentle Marian Lane, cold-eyed Marian Lane. But there is another side, I suspect."

"What other side?"

"They never have seen her with ghosts in her eyes, as I have; they never have watched her slip like a graceful cat at night across the roof of Pete's Place. What would they say to that? What would all the honest boys say?"

"That I am a seeker after truth, if they only knew."

"Truth is fire," said he. "I've come here tonight to beg for a truce. You see that I don't stand on pride. I beg for forgiveness, and forgetfulness. I've come all this distance to see you and ask you to be a friend, instead of an enemy. Do you believe that?"

"Why, in part," said she. "And was it in part to

see Dick Kinkaid, the man-hunter? I'm sorry the dance is over. That's where I want to sit—over in that corner—"

It was Kinkaid's corner, and toward it he took her, realizing that the appeal had gone unanswered and that it was indeed war to the knife. But now he was before Kinkaid. He could hear the last word on the lips of excellent Colonel Hope—and they were something about that ghoul of a man, Larry Jude.

Then he stood before Kinkaid, and a great hand of iron closed over his with unnecessary force, until he raised his head.

So, for the first time, each looked into the eyes of the other, steadily, remorselessly, never giving way until a longer pause would have called attention upon them.

The next dance started; and away went Marian Lane in the arms of the great Kinkaid. She was talking to him now, as eagerly as he to her.

"You know this Duval pretty well?" he had asked her.

"*I* don't know him at all," said she. "But he's wonderful, isn't he?"

"Humph!" grunted Kinkaid.

"And how I should like to know who Duval really is!" said she.

"Would you?" answered Kinkaid. "Then I'll tell you that you're going to, and going to hear the facts from me! He's got an eye in his head, for one thing!

11

The cream of a country dance is always the last of it, when the older people who give it sanction and dignity have gone home, and the orchestra has played itself into some degree of abandon, and the crowd that is left is thinking of nothing but the joy of motion.

Pretty Marian Lane was still there, as though she had no store to open in the morning. Strange to say, big Kinkaid also lingered, and the late dancers almost forgot to look at him with awe. It was almost as remarkable a thing that Duval was also present.

He was everywhere.

He danced only that once with Marian Lane. After that, he was interested in turn in every girl present, as it seemed, for he danced with each, and between dances he appeared to discover great interest and charm in round-backed old grandmothers who sat along the wall as chaperones.

He was not with the women alone, but also in the anteroom—once reserved for saddles and such gear in the days of the barn's real usefulness—where he found the men between dances hastily smoking cigarettes. He lounged and talked with these; he walked up and down with young Charles Nash, arm in arm, and Charlie obviously proud of this distinction which was given to him. He submitted, also, to a good deal of bantering upon the obvious pleasure which he was getting from the dance.

"He wants somebody at his stove besides a man to cook," said a cheerful cowpuncher, "and so he's come out here to find somebody. He's a doggone practical man, ain't you, Duval? When you go to get yourself a woman, you take my advice and practice up a mite on runnin'—for safety's sake! But why ain't you ever come out before?"

Duval explained that he would have been pleased enough to do so. But he had to work. The farm was young. It needed infinite care. But he at last had a great idea. He was going to raise asparagus and make a fortune!

They listened to him with their eyes upon the floor. It was not the first extravagant scheme he had hatched. Once he was going to buy lean young cattle from the southern drives as they came north toward the grasslands in the summer and put them in sheds to be fattened.

Now he had struck asparagus, and the cowpunchers bit their lips to keep from smiling, until Duval heard the orchestra begin and hurried off to find a partner.

"How does he keep goin', Charlie?" said one. "He ain't made a cent out of that fool farm, and he's spendin' all the time at a terrible rate!"

"I dunno," said Charlie. "But he told me once about a terrible fine evenin' that he had at roulette up Montana way, before he quit the T Bar place. And I reckon that's why he's still flush. Spendin' his capital on you and me and all the other boys, and never complainin' because he don't get nothin' back. Why, boys, God Almighty send Duval a woman with a business head that'll take charge of him!"

Murphy laughed, and others joined him.

"Who'll take charge of Duval?" they asked. And Charlie Nash agreed with them, half sadly and half with a fierce pride.

"I seen him stand up and look Kinkaid in the eye," said he. "There wasn't no backin' up. Kinkaid seemed like he'd been hit with a lead pipe. He wasn't used to havin' gents eye him that way!"

They chuckled. The whole range was proud of its new champion, rejoiced in his valor, liked him for his kindness, admired him for his wisdom, and loved him for his folly!

But what they did not understand at all was the thing that Marian Lane suggested to Charlie Nash, as they were dancing together still later that morning. He had gone over the great good points of his friend as a disciple and a worshipper, in an outburst from the heart.

"Of course," said the girl, "but suppose that he's thought out all these things before? Suppose that the farm's only a blind, and the other things all done for a game? *I* don't think that anyone in the world could ever have been such an idiot as to plan to fatten cattle on cabbages; certainly not a smart whip like Duval. You can think what you please, but I know that he's laughing at us a lot more than we're laughing at him."

She compressed her lips a little and waited for Charlie's explosion of wrath. It followed at once.

"I never seen such a poison-mean nature like

you got, Marian! Everything you don't understand, you're agin."

At this moment a loud voice ran into the room shouting: "Where's Marshal Kinkaid? Where's Dick Kinkaid?"

The messenger blundered across the floor, and finding Kinkaid in his corner, bellowed: "Mr. Kinkaid, hell's poppin'. They've cracked the safe of Broom and Carson and they've got clean away with a hundred and eighty thousand dollars which there was inside of it! They've got clean off and nobody knows how they've gone or who they might be except that one of them had hurt himself in the hand and left some blood marks—"

Kinkaid took his informant under his arm, as it were, and departed from the room with him. Duval disappeared at the same instant. He headed back across the hills toward his home as fast as a horse could trot between the shafts of Simon Wilbur's borrowed buggy.

At Wilbur's he hastily stowed the buggy, and led the horse back to its own corral; then went softly down the path to the cabin.

The front door was open, as was their custom in all except the windiest weather; so Duval walked freely in and found old Henry asleep, smiling at his dreams.

"Henry!" he called. "The sun's up, and the cow is waiting for you at the bars."

"Hello," said Henry, "how was the fourteen-carat marshal, and did you bring home his watch and chain or wasn't there even that left of him, when you got through?"

"Did you think that I went there to fight him?" asked Duval. "I went there to let him see me and to try a game of bluff."

"That worked? I never seen a better poker face than yours, in a pinch."

"Nothing works with Kinkaid," said Duval frankly.

"Not lame nowhere?" asked Henry, sitting up with a yawn.

"The girl?" murmured Duval suddenly. "Is that a chance? I wonder!" He added: "How was the night with you, Henry?"

"Lonely, a little. I took a walk."

"As far as what?"

"Oh, up and over a coupla hills. That's all. Then I come home and I'm asleep before I know it. I'm getting old, I tell you."

"Ay," said Duval sternly, "you're getting old."

"Now what's the matter?" asked Henry.

"When a man's hands begin to slip, it's time for him to call himself old. Let me see yours!"

"What's the lead?" barked Henry angrily. "Because I barked my hand opening that fool of a latch on the gate when I come home—"

"You rattle-headed bungler!" said Duval. "You drivelling out-of-date cracker of penny banks for children! You've left your blood on the Broom and Carson safe, and Kinkaid is going to run down the trail to my house and snag us both!"

It was a long and jagged rip on the inside of the left forefinger. Duval bathed it in hot salt water until Henry's face wrinkled with pain. Then he dressed it with care, making the bandage as secure as possible, but also as thin.

"There'll be no trouble," said Henry reassuringly. "I've tore my finger on that sharp notch under the latch. What's wrong with that?"

"Kinkaid!" said Duval. "Robbery or no robbery, he'd come here anyway to see me. And you live with me, Henry, I suppose?"

He added: "What the devil made you do it, after I'd warned you?"

"It was the face of that safe that kept looking in on me," confessed Henry. "I went to bed and put out the light. I was ready to go to sleep. I *was* asleep, when I seen the safe like the face of a friend, winking at me. Pretty soon I was in the saddle on Cherry, and humping it over the hills—"

"Cherry?" groaned Duval.

"Why not? What else? The mule?"

"Why not? Because there's nothing like Cherry on the whole range!"

"She didn't talk," grinned Henry, "going or coming."

"She had to step on the ground, though!" said Duval.

Henry stared in consternation.

"What did you do with her when you got there?"

"Tied her in a clump of poplars about a furlong from the finish."

"That's better," nodded Duval. "Did you leave any fingerprints in that blood?"

"I wiped every mark. Didn't have time to get all of the blood away, but every mark was wiped over."

He chuckled.

"Here," said he, as Duval finished bandaging the finger. "Here's the stuff."

He started to raise the thin straw pallet from his bunk but Duval stopped him with a word.

"I don't want to see it!"

"Hey, what?" demanded Henry, amazed. "It won't hurt your eyes. You get your percentage, anyway—"

Duval raised one finger.

"How long have you known me, Henry?"

"Twenty years, sir. Nineteen, to be on the dotted line."

"Did you ever see me mix drinks?"

"No, sir."

"What am I?"

"The champion—"

"Farmer?"

Henry grinned.

"I'll eat the crops you raise," said he.

"But am I a farmer?"

"You have the look and the lingo when you want to put it on."

"I mean that I'm a farmer and nothing else. If that satchel of yours were filled with select diamonds, I wouldn't have as much use for them as I would for ten pounds of oats. If Kinkaid isn't here before the morning's over, I don't know men and their faces. Go get the shotgun and start hunting."

"Hunting what, sir?"

"I don't care what. Go and shoot a few cartridges at the air, if you want to, but don't come back till noon. Is that all clear?"

"Clear as glass, sir. I'll tell you how it was. The thin steel plate on the outside of the—"

"I don't care a whit how you cut your finger. The point is that the thing was done. Now get out of here and take your boodle with you. Hide it wherever you like. Go try to find the rabbits with that gun of yours. Start moving and move fast. You're trying to shoot some sort of meat for us. You understand? Go on, Henry. You can have breakfast and lunch together, when you come back. Take some hardtack in your pocket. Now get out!"

Duval, after he had gone, started his breakfast, stripped, and ran for a plunge in the icy brook. He came back from this well wakened and keyed for the day—dressed while he ate—and before the sun was lifted high enough to begin warming the earth, he was out with horse and mule running a small, heavy harrow over the ploughed ground in the lower meadow, while a dozen blackbirds followed critically, watching for worms and grubs.

The air was still cool, but warm enough to redouble the fragrance of the pines, when he heard the hoofbeats of a horse pause at his gate, and then saw the lofty form of Marshal Richard Kinkaid coming up the path between the fields.

He appeared to even better advantage now than he had done the night before. He wore a loose, unbuttoned coat of a dull plaid, a blue shirt with a bandanna knotted about the throat, the knot at the back of the neck and the red dappled silk flowing down over his breast. His gun belt sagged far down over the right thigh, where it supported a long holster whose black surfacing had been worn to a shining brown in most places. But above all the massive form the marshal was crowned and completed by the high sombrero which he wore in the Mexican style.

Kinkaid did not shake hands. He waved the glove briefly, instead.

"You don't take days off, Duval," he commented. "Dance all night—work all day!"

Cheerful, friendly words, but spoken without the slightest softening of features.

"Same to you," said Duval. "You been Carson

and Brooming, I guess?"

The marshal responded obliquely: "Hired men ain't their own masters."

"You had breakfast?"

"No."

"Come up and I'll give you a handout."

The lips of the marshal parted, and then closed.

"No," he said. "I gotta take off weight; I'm gettin' too fat for the hosses that I can buy. But I'd like to have a talk with you, and set down a minute." Plainly his first impulse had been acquiescence.

"Sure," said Duval.

Before they went in, Kinkaid paused in front of the veranda step and turned his grim, handsome face toward the bubbling of the river, and then to the banks of foliage which hedged in the farm.

"Quiet, here," he remarked. "You could hear yourself think, in this here place, Duval."

"Ay," said Duval, "there ain't many comes up the road, excepting Wilbur. Go on in."

He pointed to his own big chair, and the marshal sat down in it. He filled it completely!

Never before in all his days had Duval seen such a body, such a face, such gleaming, steady eyes which laid a weight instantly upon him.

"Coffee, anyway," said Duval.

"Coffee?" repeated the other, his eyes flashing hungrily toward the big blackened pot upon the stove. Then he shook his head. "I don't need anything," he declared.

To Duval, closely watching, it appeared undoubted that the marshal had felt some obscure qualm of conscience, and if he had guessed at once that the visit was not altogether friendly, his last doubt was now removed, definitely.

The esteem which he felt for the physical and mental powers of the marshal was not without some return, he was soon aware, for though Kinkaid managed to cover much under a casual manner, still there was a question and a faint doubt in his eyes, such as appears when a man is not entirely sure of his surroundings.

"You been up at the Broom and Carson place, I suppose?" said Duval again, purposely taking up the question which was most in his mind.

"Yeah, I been there."

"That's a cleanup," said Duval thoughtfully. "You take a cleanup like that, it's worth while."

"In a penitentiary, what good does it do the crook?" asked Kinkaid.

"Why not? Maybe he gets fifteen years. Good behavior and he's out in ten," said Duval. "Well, when he's out, he goes back to the place where he's cached the coin, picks it out of the ground, and he's fixed for the rest of his life. Ten years down, and everything else on credit is pretty soft, I'd tell a man!"

"Some of them figure it that way," said the marshall without interest. "This was an old hand, though, and nobody young enough to want to risk ten years in jail."

"Old fellow, eh?" asked Duval, bright with interest.

"Yeah. Pretty old, I reckon."

"Well, doggone me if I see how you tell his age," said Duval, as one prepared to admire brilliance beyond his own scope.

"Well, he didn't have too much time on his

hands but everything he done was neat. Laid the drawers and trays out in rows, and didn't ruffle everything up. A young crook leaves a messy job. The old boys, they're likely to have a sort of a pride in appearances, if you foller my drift!"

"Sure," agreed Duval. "I could see how that might be. Still, you might be wrong?"

"Maybe. Anyway, I'll have him before long."

He paused, letting his eyes rather covertly drift about the room.

"You done a pile of dancing in your time," said Kinkaid, apropos of nothing.

"I done some when I was a kid."

"You can step," said the marshal absently.

And suddenly he was looking at Duval with an open, flaming envy in his eyes, so extremely patent that Duval had to look out of the door in order to avoid appearing to recognize it.

"Partly," went on the marshal, shrugging his heavy shoulders, "I come here on business. I've heard that you got a mare that can outrun the jack rabbits."

"She's fast," admitted Duval, without enthusiasm.

"In my line," said Kinkaid, "I need a fast one. I'd aim to buy that mare, Duval."

"Would you?" said Duval. "But she ain't for sale; besides, she wouldn't carry your weight, I reckon."

"I'd like to see her. Maybe I could make you an offer."

Duval did not hesitate. There was not apt to be a man in the West who would refuse to offer his horse to the admiration of even the most casual passer-by, let alone such a celebrity as Kinkaid. He went out at once with the big man and took him to the pasture.

She was grazing on the far side, and at the whistle of her master she tossed her head and came to him with her long, bounding stride. Kinkaid looked at her with a critical eye.

"Rawhide and catgut!" said he. "She's twice what she looks. She could carry me, Duval!"

"Maybe, Kinkaid, but don't you go tempting me. I like that mare a lot!"

"I'll tell you," said the marshal. "Without no trial, without lookin' her over, I'll pay you down five hundred spot cash for her!"

It was a large price, almost a staggering price on a range where a tough mustang, broken to the saddle, could be bought for fifty dollars, and in Mexico for less.

Duval, entrenched in his part, saw that he must appear to be tempted, and he said: "It's a lot of money, Kinkaid. But look here. I was flush last winter and had a bust clean to New York. I saw a horse show there and she done fine, the way she slid over the jumps. I couldn't get her out of my head. So I sent and got her when I was flush again. It cost me a lot of money and a lot of thinkin', too."

"Well," said Kinkaid impatiently, "lemme try her, will you?"

"Sure."

Kinkaid brought up his own saddle from the powerful animal he had been riding, and this was cinched on the back of the mare; then the marshal mounted. He simply jogged her down to the bottom of the path, then turned her and galloped her back to the pasture at full speed.

His eyes gleamed as he dismounted, but his deep voice was quiet as he said: "A thousand dollars, Duval! You gotta have more acres. You can get 'em with this money. Take a gent like you that'll be marryin' before long, he's gotta have more land than this to keep a wife, and maybe kids!"

"Yeah," agreed Duval grudgingly. "But look here, Kinkaid. They's some things that you can't get with money. Suppose that you seen a man with a fine son. Would you put a price on the kid?"

"Suppose I wanted him, why not? Suppose that I could give the kid a fine home, and everything that he wanted, and a reputation—why, I'd make this here mare famous, Duval."

He added: "I'll come up a little. I'll give you twelve hundred iron men for her!"

Duval shook his head.

"Oh," said Kinkaid. "Money don't mean much to you, eh? Maybe I was wrong. I thought that you was a small farmer, Duval! Maybe you're just a banker takin' a vacation?"

At this slowly drawled suspicion, Duval felt himself weaken. Certainly his own attitude was going to be hard to understand if he held out much longer. But he knew it was not merely for the pursuit of criminals that the other wanted the horse. He had some purpose in the back of his mind which was not to the advantage of the present owner of the mare, though what that purpose could be, Duval was unable to decipher.

"I'll make you a last price," said the marshal. "I want her, and I figger that I ought to have her. What good is she to you? She ain't for ploughin'. You don't often go out, except down to the village,

I reckon. She's nothin' to you but something to look at—and I'll pay you fifteen hundred cash on the nail for her!"

Cold sweat burst out on Duval; he was silenced and sick.

"That," went on Kinkaid, "is what you give for your house and your whole farm. You can have twice as much of a farm, now. If farmin' is what you're really interested in!"

"No," said Duval, "I can't let her go!"

But he said it faintly, for he realized that this refusal would make his whole position seem absurd.

Kinkaid did not appear to have heard the refusal. He had taken out a long fat, pigskin wallet and unfolding this, he drew out a stack of bills, oddly neat and crisp. From them he took two five-hundred dollar notes, and after these, some of smaller denominations. He packed the stack together, and offered it to Duval, who reached for it, hesitated, and then took it in his hand with another speech of refusal on his lips.

The marshal, however, seemed to take the conclusion of the affair for granted.

He turned to the mare and looked her over almost spitefully now, scowling at her long legs and skinny, reaching neck.

"She's pretty lean," he objected. "I'd like to put fifty pounds on her, but I reckon that she's one of them skinny devils that never get fat. Here you, Cherry, stand still!"

He raised his voice loudly as he delivered the order. The ears of the mare flattened but she was still.

"I'm late," said Kinkaid. "Here—sign this. It ain't very regular, but it'll do for a bill of sale, maybe."

And he placed before Duval a slip of paper which read: "For value received I, the undersigned, have sold the chestnut mare called Discretion to Richard Kinkaid."

Duval had been trapped, and sign he must, so the pen slowly traced his name—"D. Duval."

He passed it back and thrust the sale money down into his coat pocket. Looking up, it seemed to him that he had surprised a faint smile upon the lips of the other.

But the thing was ended; the mare was gone; and Kinkaid was riding her down toward the gate!

12

What is more stifling than for a strong and brave man to be forced to control his anger? So it was that Duval choked with his wrath as he looked down the path after the marshal.

Cherry was gone forever!

Such a procession of pictures then passed through his mind as had not been in it for many a day, for he was seeing all the days and the ways of Cherry from her spring days as a foal to her wild days as a two-year-old, when she had been tried for the track and found just short of the right foot, and then the dark days of her three-year-old form, when she was neither hunter nor racer, but simply a long striding hack, pleasant to drift with across the countryside. In those days, their affection for one another had become fixed. He rode her not because he valued her, but because he loved her wise, ugly head and her imperial ways, and she loved him as only a good horse can. In her fourth year began her glory; and this was her fifth.

But now she was taken out of his hand by the coin and the cunning of Kinkaid, lost to him forever; and he actually had signed the document that divided them!

There was less security for Kinkaid's future at that moment than there ever had been before!

Kinkaid himself had ridden down to the village, and there he stopped in front of the grocery store to buy some dried meat for his food supply. Not that he needed the meat, but he wished to accomplish a double outside purpose. One was to allow the people of Moose Creek to see what he had done; the other was to personally inform Miss Marian Lane.

The crowd gathered the instant the marshal appeared on the chestnut, but for the moment he had enough to do in meeting the girl.

She finished serving a customer, but her eyes and her smile were both for Kinkaid as he strode toward the counter. And then she saw the mare tethered in the street just as he gave his order.

It was the sweetest pleasure to Kinkaid to see the consternation, almost the fear, in her face.

"You borrowed her!" she gasped in explanation.

"I bought her," said the marshal. "I needed a fast hoss, so I bought her. I want two pounds of dried beef and a pound of hardtack."

She went to fill the order.

"Poor Duval!" she said as she brought the order to him and wrapped it up. "Poor Duval! Is he as broke as that?"

But he saw, with relief, that it was not real pity that was in her voice, but merely the semblance of it; really, there was sheer excitement, and she looked at him as though he had accomplished some wonderful thing, far beyond the mere purchase of a horse. She, too, knew that Duval had been vanquished, and the thought made her eyes shine.

And the heart of the marshal was filled with surety and with peace. He had thought, the night before, that Duval had danced his way into the very heart of the girl. He assured himself now that there was no fear whatever of that danger.

"You paid, then," said she.

"Fifteen hundred," said the marshal carelessly.

He did not look at her as he gathered up his parcel, but he knew that he had made a point, and a great one. Such a sum of money as this was not spent, in that range, for the sake of a riding horse!

But then he went out hastily. He knew that he could not make effects by mere conversation. His role with her must be that of the man of action, who performs three deeds to every sentence that he speaks.

From the crowd, too, he received the same murmur of wonder.

Pete came out from his saloon, wiping his hands on his white apron, and gaped like a child at the mare and her new rider.

"Borrowed?"

"Bought!" said the marshal.

"My God," said Pete, "poor Duval! Is he gone bust, already?"

But Charlie Nash, dark with doubt, shook his head.

"They's something behind it," he said to himself. "They's gunna be trouble. They's gunna be big trouble! They's gunna be trouble which Moose Creek never seen the like."

The marshal, content, went out of town with the long striding mare half-extended, swaying him forward, even then, at an amazing speed, and in this gait he held her for mile after mile; he sprinted her up a sharp slope, and at the top of it reined her in and listened carefully to her breathing. She was well covered with sweat, but then the day was warm; her breathing was slow and easy, and she went up well against the bit, plain token that she was fit for further effort. So Kinkaid drew in a breath so deep that it crowded his shoulders back and made him sit the saddle like a conqueror returning from the battlefield. He felt, in fact, that the battle already was won, that he had demonstrated his superiority over Duval in this entire transaction, that he had staggered the faith of Moose Creek in its hero, and that he had fixed the attention of Marian Lane upon himself.

As for Duval, it seemed patent to the marshal that the mare was not too expensive even at fifteen hundred dollars. How much had Duval paid for her, then? Why did he let her go at no profit, or even at a loss? Obviously, simply to maintain his role as the simple farmer of no resources. That role, then, was a farce, and something more than the eye perceived lay behind Duval. That, then, was the reason that Marian Lane had begged him to find out more about the stranger at Moose Creek.

The marshal literally laughed aloud, for he began to see that this was not only a woman for his heart but also a companion for his brain. She was one who would know his problems, understand them enough to give keen feminine suggestions, here and there, above all, enough to admire the talent which he expended in his labors!

He wakened from his daydream with a start to find himself almost in the act of riding past the Broom and Carson place. He turned in hastily, biting his lip, and straightway began his investigation.

To the amazement of the distressed Mr. Carson, who was frantically walking up and down inside, the celebrated marshal paid not the slightest heed to the interior of the shop, but he went out to a certain patch of poplar trees which he had located when he first looked for signs around the place.

There had found the grass trampled, and leading from the trees back into the woods, there were more hoof marks in the grass. They had been made by a trotting horse, and the length of the stride was what had made him think at once of Duval's mare, now celebrated on the range for her long action.

He trotted the mare in a parallel course, but when he dismounted for measurement, he discovered that the slipping of the hoofs in the grass and the fact that the grass trampled down in the morning already was springing up straight again, made it impossible for him to make any accurate measurements for comparison.

He looked next down the back trail striving to find a distinct print of a hoof, but that was almost equally difficult.

There were plenty of dim impressions upon dead pine needles, there were scratches on rocky surfaces, but there were no real prints. He had been working for at least an hour in this patient fashion, getting no results, when he was aware that he was being watched from behind his back, and turning sharply about, he saw a tall man with a gloomy face—a big savage whose thin lips were hooked in the curve of a perpetual sneer.

"Hello!" said Kinkaid. "What are you lookin' at, stranger."

"I'm lookin' at a man waste his time, Kinkaid," said the other.

The marshal took no immediate offence.

"Can you do better at this job?" he asked.

"Tolerable," said the other.

"That's what you say."

For a reply, the other carelessly raked the pine needles before his foot.

"Look here," said he.

The marshal obediently went to look, and there he found the complete and delicate outline of a near forefoot, the very nail holes being clearly indicated.

"That's what you want, I reckon?" said the stranger.

The marshal, without an answer, brought up the mare at once, and caused her to step with her left forefoot exactly beside the former mark.

The instant the impression was made there was no need for measurement. The two were identical to the spacing of the nail holes! There was the same rather large spread of hoof, the same distance between the open ends of the shoe—in all respects the two were identical, and it was established that moment beyond cavil that this mare, earlier in the morning, had been ridden to the poplars, held there long enough to trample the grass down, and then brought back through the trees.

"Duval was at the dance," said the marshal. "Who are his friends in Moose Creek? Because I got an idea that one of 'em is a fellow with a hurt hand, just now."

"They's an old man named Henry that lives with him," said the stranger.

"Tell me," said the marshal with interest. "Who

are you? If you got eyes as good as this, I could use you, friend, and pay you good for your time, too."

"I got no use for money on this job," replied the other sourly. "I'm in it for the sake of doin' what I can to Duval. My name is Larry Jude!"

13

The conclusions of the marshal were prompt, definite, and strong. Mr. Henry, as he learned, had accompanied the mare from the East. Since Duval in person could not have committed the robbery, and since the mare was most apparently ridden by the robber, therefore Henry was the guilty man.

He did not go in the daytime. He went after dark to Duval's house. It was not by the gate on the road that he approached, but from the side, cautiously squirming his way through the hedge of shrubbery, now advancing with the season into big leaf.

He had tethered his new mare fully half a mile away lest she should whinny as she approached her former home.

Once inside the hedge, he took careful account of his bearings. Before him were several fences surrounding the corral and the strawstack, which leaned in a lopsided manner toward the south under the pressure of occasional north winds.

He went deliberately to the first fence, and slipped between the bars, crossed it, and was going through the strawstack enclosure, when the whistle of a quail from the hedge disturbed him.

He flattened himself against the strawstack and whirled, gun in hand, as though enemies were already charging upon him. But then he heard the call repeated, and a distinct, though soft, rustling of the foliage far behind him.

He analyzed the notes of the whistle with care, but it was the perfect call! Four short notes in a quick ripple, and after the last a slight break in the rhythm and the final touch.

Yet the marshal waited, to make surety doubly sure. He knew that he was now invisible, pressed as he was against the side of the stack. He felt the chaff work loose, and stream down inside his shirt collar, working deep against his skin.

However, in spite of this discomfort he remained for a long time in this manner, motionless. Then he started again for the house, but not in a straight line. He first got out of the strawstack enclosure, and stole down toward the side of the horse shed, inside of which he heard the horse and the mule nosing at the sweet hay, and stamping with content. From the shed he then angled up on a new course toward the cabin.

From a new line, therefore, he went on toward the house, all because a quail had been disturbed in the hedge behind him and given bobwhite's familiar call! On this new line, he went with a redoubled caution, stooping very low, so that no one would be apt to see him from any point of view against the radiance of the lighted window, no matter how dim. Fairly creeping, now, he slipped toward the house, bending so low that he touched the ground before him with the tips of his fingers, and so explored it more accurately than with a light to make sure that his following footfall would make no noise.

STRANGE COURAGE 117

His attention was by no means confined to the house which drew closer and closer, but now and again he paused and scanned everything around him, to either side and to the rear.

When he made these pauses, however, he could hardly have been expected to see the form that slid behind him and, when he paused, stopped also, disappearing against the flat blackness of the ground by lying face down.

So the marshal went on until he was in touching distance of the house itself.

All was still, inside, except for two sounds, each wonderfully faint but perceptible by his keen ear. One was the singing of a kettle on the stove, and the other was the occasional soft crackle of paper, as though the pages of a large book were being turned. One of the two was doubtless in bed—hence the lack of conversation. The other sat immersed in his book, allowing something to cook on the late fire.

Kinkaid stood up straight. He was now close against the wall of the house, so that this background would prevent him from being seen at a distance of more than a few paces. He stood up, and as he did so, something cold and very hard was laid against the back of his neck.

"Hoist your hands," said Duval's voice.

The marshal, for a moment, was speechless. In that first dreadful flash of apprehension, it seemed to him that he could hear Duval's quietly regretful voice stating how the lurking form had approached his house, how he hailed—challenged—fired—

And so the end of famous Richard Kinkaid, obscurely shot!

He could not speak; he could only slowly obey the command.

"Wait a minute," said Duval. "I see you're hitched up to a gun. Unbuckle that belt, stranger, and do it slow, and don't try to turn, because if you do, you'll turn into a ghost. Salt that idea away, partner!"

"Duval," began Kinkaid, "I'm Richard Kinkaid and—"

"And I'm Napoleon," said Duval pleasantly. "Sure. I understand! Let that belt drop and the gun with it, or you'll be Kinkaid no more!"

The marshal did not hesitate. The firm, cold pressure against the nape of his neck spoke to him in a more penetrating manner than words could ever do.

He unbuckled his gun belt, and the gun and the cartridges above it dropped with a solid thump to the ground. For the first time in his mature days, the famous marshal was unarmed!

"Now we'll have those hands up good and high," said Duval. "Think what mama told you. Stretch yourself and try to pick a star out of the sky, and sashay right around the house and go in through the front door, big boy! Walk slow and easy, and don't stumble if you love your life!"

So Kinkaid gained the door, and strode rather awkwardly into the room.

At the exact center of it, he halted. His fingertips were touching the low ceiling, and willingly he would have pulled down that ceiling upon himself and his captor.

Yet another thought came into his mind—the consternation of Duval when at last he should know who his prisoner was in point of fact.

He heard Duval saying: "You can turn around,

·keepin' your hands still restin' on the ceilin', partner."

So the marshal turned, slowly as he had been ordered, and stood eye to eye with Duval.

The latter stared at him without amazement, with a keen and curious interest.

"Well, Kinkaid," said he, "I can see that folks don't do right by you, callin' you a pretty stern and gloomy gent; here I find you playin' hide-and-seek. What were you playin' with, Kinkaid? You can tell me while you put your hands down!

"Speakin' personal," went on Duval. "I always liked to see a gent that would get out and join the kids and be jolly. But I couldn't tell whether you was playin' hide-and-seek, or sneakin' up to rob a hen roost, or what. Robbin' hen roosts was a favorite game of mine when I was a kid. Did you ever do it, Kinkaid?"

"Duval," said the marshal gravely, "you've made a tolerable fool out of me. It's up to me to tell you why I'm here, though, and I'll do it. I'm here because I came for your hired man—Henry. Where is he?"

"Henry? You want Henry? Don't tell me, Kinkaid, that you want to play hide-and-seek with Henry, because he never could run fast enough to make you enjoy the game!"

"Are you gunna keep this up?" asked Kinkaid sourly. "D'you know who you're talkin' to?"

"Why, Dick," said Duval, "I guess that I'm pretty nigh the only man in Moose Creek that really knows you, and the playful way you got with you. Other folks wouldn't hardly believe it possible that you been up here and visited me and played hide-

and-seek, this way! And with old Henry, too! They'll sure be a pile amused by that. Everybody from Pete the bartender to Marian Lane."

The last name was a thrust at the very vitals of the marshal's pride.

He swallowed hard.

"Duval," said he, "I ain't to think that you're gunna try to spread the news of this here around?"

"Why," said Duval, "I wouldn't think of talkin' about the game, at all. I wouldn't be dreamin' of it. Because most likely all idea of it will drop out of my head! I'll forget it, complete, and I'll ask Henry if he won't forget it, too!"

He whistled, imitating beautifully the call of the quail chick, repeated it, and eventually there was the sound of a footstep outside the house. Henry appeared in the doorway with an apprehensive look on his face.

"What d'you think, Henry?" said Duval. "The marshal's been up here to play hide-and-seek with you. Like he wanted to tag you, only he got tagged first, and we was both wonderin' if we could forget about it, if the marshal, say, was to forget about your bad finger."

Henry stared violently.

"By the Lord!" said the marshal through his teeth. "It *was* the old man! What're you tryin' to do, Duval? Blackmail me to keep me silent? You fool, I'll have you both in jail before the world's a day older!"

"Jail!" said Duval, flashing a smile at the larger man. "Why, that'd sure wake us up and make us talk, Kinkaid. I figger that everybody would be mighty interested, too, to hear about how Richard Kinkaid, he come slippin' along in the dark, like he was after chickens on the roost—"

"I see what you're drivin' at," said Kinkaid. "You think I'll shut up sooner than have you talk. You jackass, what difference does it make to me what you say? Will people believe you against me?"

Duval took from behind his back the cartridge belt and the gun.

"Maybe they wouldn't believe me," he said in a soothing voice. "And they'd think that I picked these up on the road, somewheres? Maybe they'd think that. A mighty disbelievin' gang we got around this here town of Moose Creek, old-timer!"

At this, as the full point of the remark came home to him, Kinkaid felt his soul shrivel like dead leaves. He was dizzy with rage, and with helplessness.

"I'll tell you, son," said Duval, "the fact is that you and me and Henry are all gunna be friends. I could sort of see it in you when I first clapped eyes on you. The sort of a gent that I'd like to have for a friend. What about you, Henry?"

"I like him right off," said Henry, grinning enormously.

"The mare, too," said Duval, and putting away his gun inside his coat with a swift gesture, he took out a wallet from which he extracted the fifteen hundred dollars which the marshal had paid him for the horse that morning. This he extended, with his left hand.

Kinkaid hesitated. It would be a simple thing to throw himself upon Duval—if only he could estimate the speed with which the latter might be able to get his gun out of his coat. Besides, there was old Henry looking grimly on, and the latter decided the marshal on passivity.

He took the money that was offered to him.

"What's it for?" he asked. "D'you want the mare back?"

"Wouldn't dream of takin' her back," said Duval, "considerin' the price that you paid for her, but the fact is that you found out during the day that she wouldn't stand up under your weight, and so that was why you come back here to see me. You wanted to know if I'd call the sale off. Wanted to know if I'd give you back the money and take the mare instead. And Duval, bein' a kind of poor businessman and a mighty good fellow, he said sure, that he'd take the mare back, and look on today as though it never had happened."

What Kinkaid saw, first of all, was the face of the girl in the store, that morning, as she had looked up to him with astonished excitement—she, his wife to be, helpmate, companion in arms, as it were. When she had seen that the mare belonged to him, it was as though she already saw Duval mastered and his problem and mystery solved.

That satisfaction would have to be surrendered. He saw all the advantages which he already had gained stripped away from him by this polite, cheerful, smiling devil, Duval! And though he strove to struggle against him, he was held by a silken thread.

For he dared not allow Duval to go abroad and show the captured revolver. It was so well known —even the appearance of a new holster in place of the famous old brown and shiny one would cause infinite comment—and the gun itself wedded to his hand these years, marked with nine small, regular, neat notches—

The marshal burst into a profuse perspiration.

"I know how it is," said Duval sympathetically. "It's a mighty big relief to get rid of a hoss that you spent so much money for, after you find out that she really ain't meant for you, as you might say. But you're busy—you're mighty busy, Kinkaid. I suppose you'll want to be hurryin' away? Can't persuade you to stay here and have a bit of something to eat with us? No?"

Kinkaid gave no answer. Shame, rage, horror overwhelmed him, and he rushed out into the night.

14

Duval, when the marshal had fled outdoors with his shame, sat down in his chair, beside which, on the table, lay an open book. Its leaves, rustled by the wind now and again, had made the comfortably domestic sound which had so lulled Kinkaid's last suspicions in approaching the place.

"You knew he'd come," said Henry, erect by the door and frowning. "I dunno how you worked that!"

"That's simple. He wouldn't have wanted the mare so badly if he hadn't had some way of connecting her with the crime. He came for her; he got her out of me, and I hated parting with her worse than blood—I hope she'll be back, soon!"

"You give him the money," said Henry, "but you paid him before you got the mare!"

"There's no danger," said Duval. "He might slip around with another gun, however, and shoot through the window—"

"Him?" gasped Henry, and jumped.

"No," said Duval. "On second thought I believe that he won't attempt anything this evening. He'll be content to return the mare to me—"

"Ay," said Henry. "That's what I thought when

he went out. He's finished and he's flat!"

"But he may come to life later on," said Duval. "He *will* come to life, in fact, and we'll have more trouble with him."

"Then let's get out!" said Henry fervently. "If you've won one stake, what's the use of betting on every race that's left on the program? Let's go home, sir!"

"What's home, then?"

"Any place on the wing. What's home for the wild geese? Going north or going south. We better do the same way, eh?"

This suggestion Duval considered quietly for a time, and then he said: "I've had the same idea, Henry, but I don't think that I can go yet. I have unfinished business—"

He paused here, and Henry watched him anxiously.

"The marshal knows!" he said, "and as long as the marshal knows, it won't be long before other folks know, too! It'll be in the air. And then we're both cooked!"

Duval shook his head.

"Kinkaid can't talk—except to us! His mouth is shut! I was getting so tired of safety, Henry, that I hated to open my eyes in the morning and look at the day coming. I was so weary of the good, quiet life, that I was almost delighted to see you come with the mare in one hand and blackmail in the other!"

Henry shrugged his lean shoulders, as he replied: "Don't know just how you've managed it, but you've kept me away from Kinkaid, and there's no blackmail in my mind now, sir. When a man gets old, he's apt to try bad lines. I'm through with that one!"

"Of course you are," said Duval. "Tell me, Henry. Don't you enjoy a time like this, when we can't tell how luck may jump against us the next moment?"

"I understand what you mean," muttered Henry. "But I've got two hundred thousand up on this race and I want to win."

"The pretty girl with the doll's face—the beauty of the grocery store—she's the tanglefoot that is most apt to catch us."

Henry waited for further light, but Duval merely added:

"Not with her own hands, but she knows how to use the hands of other people. I would rather have three Kinkaids to deal with than one Marian Lane. How can she be handled? I don't know! That's the problem!"

He began to pace the floor.

"Here's the marshal," he said, holding up the celebrated Colt with its notches. "I have him in my hand. I suppose he'll say that his gun is in the repairer's hands! But suppose that I should put this gun on the bar of Pete's Place—why, the reputation of Dick Kinkaid would burn up like a match in no time! And he understands that."

He went on more slowly: "The sheriff is a good-natured old fellow. He may have a few doubts about me, but he's willing to put his doubts in his pocket. He doesn't need to be counted in unless fighting should begin, and then he's as dangerous as the next man. That leaves only the girl with her eternal question: Who is Duval?"

He broke off short, saying: "How the devil is one to handle a woman like that, Henry?"

"Money—" began Henry.

"Don't be a fool!" said the other tersely.

"I dunno," said Henry. "When I was a youngster I never found any way of getting along with a woman unless she happened to be in love with me. And when she was, then she was a doggone nuisance."

Duval stopped in his pacing and raised his pale face in thought.

"Love!" said he. "I hadn't thought about that! Love!"

He laughed as he spoke, but he was filled with excitement.

"Suppose, Henry, that I can keep the sheriff quiet, the great Kinkaid muzzled, and put the girl in my pocket, so to speak. That would be the hardest thing I ever tried to do. Three balls all in the air at the same time, and never falling! What do you say, Henry?"

"Hello!" exclaimed the other. "You mean to make her think—"

"That I can't keep away from her. That she's upset me completely. That I lie awake at night thinking of Marian Lane. That Marian Lane is closer to my heart than my left elbow!"

"Well?"

"Why, nothing, except that it may get me what I've wanted to have—a quiet summer here!"

15

Old Henry, his left hand in his coat pocket and his right hand carrying an envelope, entered the grocery store in the sleepy quiet of the mid-afternoon to find Marian Lane asleep in a chair behind the counter.

She tipped forward to her feet, shook the sleep out of her pretty head, and accepted the envelope with a smile.

The letter it contained read:

Dear Miss Lane,
 I'd like to talk to you, and the place I'd pick wouldn't have even walls to listen. Will you give me the chance and say where? Henry will take back your answer.

David Duval

Beneath this, she scribbled instantly:

 I'm going for a walk up the creek in about ten minutes, and since it goes past your door, I suppose we could meet on the way?

This she returned to Henry, and watched him

out of the store. Then she hurried up the stairs to change.

She never dressed more rapidly, and never with more care.

When she had finished, she stood for another moment in profound thought, rubbing her fingers a little deeper into the tight fingers of her wash gloves. She seemed to be reviewing the weapons with which she was going afield, and finding at last that they were in fair order and of a sufficient number, she passed the tip of a finger across her forehead to make all lines of reflection vanish and went lightly down the stairs and out to the street.

So she entered the woodland trail and walked along it none too briskly. By this time, she reasoned that Duval must have been waiting for her fifteen or twenty minutes, so that he must have been brought to a desirable state of mind; a little more waiting, however, would do him no harm, and above all she wished to be composed when she met him, for she felt that a duel was to take place in which she must present her sharpest wits.

What was of the utmost importance was that the mare had been returned to Duval by the marshal. He had said that the horse could not stand up under his weight, but she, having seen Cherry flaunt down the street with Kinkaid in the saddle, felt that she knew better. She could not be sure, but something told her that there had been an occurrence between Duval and the marshal in which the former came out the victor. If he could handle Kinkaid, it seemed probable that he could handle any man. As for the women—ah, that was a different matter!

Here the path turned with the bank of the creek,

and she saw Duval sitting on a rock with one knee embraced by his hands, as he stared at the water.

"Hello!" said she.

"Hello!" said Duval, standing up. "I'm delighted that you came!"

Her head tilted a little to one side, and she laughed at him.

"You've left the cowboy talk behind, I see?"

"I've left Duval over yonder in the cabin," said he. "I'm David—Castle."

"It's a nice name," said she.

"I hoped you'd like it better. Shall we walk or sit?"

"I'd rather walk, I think, David Castle."

They went up the path together at a pleasant pace, she apparently only attentive to the trees about them, the bright shrubs, and the lantern rays of sunlight that twinkled on the ground before them or glittered in the upper foliage; but in fact she knew each time he touched her with his eyes, and where the touch had fallen as distinctly as though his hand had gone out to her dusty shoes, or her swinging stick, or the flowers at her throat, or the red of her lips.

Duval, in the meantime, was in no haste to begin. But after a time he said: "How long can you be away?"

"An hour, I suppose. Then I'll have to get back to the store."

At that, he answered: "Then I'll have to start. It will take me the better part of an hour, I should say!"

"For what?" she asked.

"Confession," said he.

She stopped short and faced him, with all her

airs and mannerisms forgotten.

"If you mean that, there's no time limit."

"Good," said he. "I've asked you to come out to hear me surrender."

She did not speak; her eyes were too busy scanning him, searching, searching.

"The going is too deep for me," said he, and smiled at her. "To begin with, I'll tell you what I intended to do. I was going to tell you a cock-and-bull yarn about my past and try to win your sympathy so that you'd send no more Larry Judes and Dick Kinkaids to look me up. Jude was enough; Kinkaid was a bad one to handle, though!"

"Was?" she said.

"For the time being," said he, cautiously, "I think that Kinkaid won't trouble me again. I suppose that you've guessed that much?"

She nodded.

"But when I saw you today," said he, "all dressed for the innocent country-girl part, so simple, so excessively sweet, turning up your eyes at me—why, then, I lost heart at once. I saw that you're too clever to be fooled, Marian."

"You make me out a bad sort of a person," she remarked.

"I make you out a dangerous one to poor fellows like myself who are made of penetrable stuff. I'll even go one step further, Marian, and tell you that I was going to play the fool and the cad wholesale by trying to make love to you."

He chuckled.

"But of course the first glimpse of you put that out of my head. You know entirely too much to be fooled by acting. That's why I'm desperately going to tell you the truth."

"The whole truth?"

"And nothing but the truth."

"Of course I haven't any real right to hear it."

"You haven't."

"You make me feel like an executioner," said she.

"You are," he answered calmly.

"Well," she said, "of course I'm curious. I'd like to hear anything you have to say."

"It will take a lot of time."

"When I'm in the middle of a good story, I can always forget time."

"Mind you, this is no story."

"Nevertheless—I'll guarantee that I'll keep everything I learn a secret."

"No, you'd better not promise that."

"You're right. I can't promise that."

"You're ready?"

"Yes."

"Then prepare yourself. It's police court stuff. I'm going to start at the beginning, as they do in books," he said. "It was all horses, country life, riding, jumping, hunting for me. School was a necessary nuisance, that was all. In the summers my father generally took me West for hunting and fishing and broncho riding. To rough up my hair, as he used to say, because a fellow whose belly had never been tucked up for lack of food will never make a man. He used to start off with me across country with rifle, ammunition, and salt. We killed our food, and if we didn't kill it, we went hungry.

"I was out of college when the break came. Father died. We expected to cut up a fat melon, but instead we found that we had a house, some books, and some horses. That was about all. I'd been the leading spender, and now I had to be the leading provider.

"Father's banking was not a business at all, we discovered. He sat in an office and did what other people told him to do. His real work was riding and hunting anything from a fox to a bear; but there's no money in that. And that was all that *I* was qualified to do. However, he had one other interest—a hobby for the evenings."

"What was that?"

"He used to fiddle about as a locksmith."

"Did you learn that trade, too, from him?"

"Inside out. That was why he loved me. He used to say that I could open any door in the world, and after his death I remembered that speech of his and decided that I'd turn it into a legacy. Do you follow my drift?"

She whirled the cane and nodded. "I suppose you decided to open doors that had money behind them?"

"That's it. And there's my story, Marian."

"That's only the beginning."

"Do you want me to go on?"

"Of course!"

"Well, perhaps you want to know how I excused myself?"

"Yes. I'd like to know that."

"I was a little younger then. Not quite so able to face the facts. So I told myself that Robin Hood had done things as bad. He took from the rich and evil. He gave to the poor and good. So I decided to begin, and I did.

"It was Arthur Burchell that I picked out first. He was a member of a mortgage ring—the fellows who make a business out of throat-cutting, and he'd cut enough throats to fill his pockets with blood money. His third wife was a gold digger and she was the one creature in the world who knew how to extract coin painlessly from him. Diamonds were her hobby. She used to wear half a million dollars' worth of 'em and very little else when she went out in public in the evening. I saw her, decided that this was fair meat, and went to rob the house that same night.

"I got to the room where they were kept. It was cold November. There was frost on the roofs. Once I skidded thirty feet into an eaves' gutter. The gutter broke the force of my fall, but the fall broke the gutter."

"Did you go clear to the ground, or land in a haystack?"

"The only stacks were chimneys. It was eleven stories to the ground. No, I didn't fall. I hung on by my hands and swung myself back to an unbroken section of the gutter. Then I climbed up the roof and got in at a skylight. I found my way down through the hotel and got to the door of the Burchells' suite. I got the lock open fairly soundlessly, and into the room where the diamonds were in their pet safe."

"Did you carry that away?"

"It weighed about two hundred pounds, I think. No, I didn't carry that, but when I tried the lock, a bell rang, the lights flashed on, and fat Arthur Burchell sat up in bed with his stomach heaving with fear. He turned loose at me with an automatic and I dived through a spray of lead for the door.

"I had sense enough to lock it behind me; the corridor held a maid and porter running toward the sound of the shooting, and I shouted 'robbers!'

once or twice, and ran as if for help. I needed help, too!"

He drew up the sleeve of his left arm and showed her a broad white dot on the bulge of the muscle of the forearm.

"Burchell had clipped me here, and I was bleeding pretty badly. But I got away over the roofs, and down to the street."

"That ended the Burchell diamonds, I suppose?"

"No. I got them, all right."

"When?"

"The same night. There's nothing that makes for sound sleep like a foiled attack. I tied up my arm and waited in view of the hotel until the lights in the Burchells' rooms went out at about four in the morning. Then I went back over the roofs in exactly the same way. I got into the room the same way, too."

"Weren't you frightened to death when you stood at the door?"

"Not the least in the world. This time I was pretty sure of myself. The door opened in an instant—I remembered it perfectly from the time before, and when I got inside, I squatted by the door and listened to Burchell's snoring, and hoped it wouldn't waken his wife. I unloosed one ray from the shutter of the dark lantern and pricked the dark here and there with it. Burchell had been having champagne to celebrate his courage and his victory; there was a little table in the middle of the room that looked like a broken iceberg—it was so covered with glassware! I let the ray sparkle in them for a minute. Then I found the fag end of a champagne bottle in the ice bucket and helped myself. It was pretty flat, but I never liked champagne with too much jump in it. I was very thirsty, you see, from the loss of blood.

"It was easy to find the electrical connection of the little jewel safe, now that I knew about it. I clipped the wires, and had the safe open in a moment. Just as I raised the lid and had sent a flash of light into the contents, Mrs. Burchell sat up and gasped. I faded onto the floor. She poked Arthur in the ribs and when he woke up, she told him that she was sure that there was a man in the room. She'd seen an outline against the stars outside the window!"

"That was a ticklish moment!" said the girl.

"It was."

"What did you do?"

"Sat still."

"And then?"

"Burchell told his wife that she was a fool and that his sleep was worth more, anyway, than her blankety diamonds. He was snoring in another moment. After a while I went around to her bed to see if she was asleep."

"Br-r-r-r!" said Marian Lane. "How did you tell?"

"By listening to her breathing. When I was sure of that I went back and took the diamonds in their soft little chamois sacks, filled my pockets and left them to have their sleep out."

"And—tell me this—when you were seen by the maid and the porter in the hall, didn't they see you clearly?"

"Very. The maid described a middle-aged man with a short black moustache for the detectives the next day, and the porter described a burly ruffian who looked like an Irish prizefighter."

"You hadn't hired them?"

"Not with a penny, but in such cases, excitement generally corrupts the faithful more thoroughly than a million dollars."

"I suppose it does. So you got off scot-free?"

"Entirely. There was only the wound in my arm. It bothered me for a while, but not as much as the man did whom I used as a fence—I mean the fellow who receives stolen goods, d'you see?"

"How did he bother you?"

"He paid me a hundred thousand for half a million worth of diamonds. And after that, he tried to blackmail me for half of the hundred thousand he had paid me!"

"Did he?"

"They have their little ways, the fences!"

"What did you do?"

"I killed him," said Duval. "I was young, new at the business, and thought he meant to do what he threatened—about disgracing me, I mean."

"You killed him! You murdered him!" She gasped it out.

And Duval, looking down at her with admiration, said: "When I see you do that, I almost think that you mean what you say!"

16

"You killed the fence," she repeated. "How?"

"In the back room of his place."

"But I mean—how?"

"Why, I simply walked in and told him to draw his gun, which he did, and then I shot him through the head. The others made a good deal of noise, but when they saw that he was really dead, they stopped shouting after me and began to loot the place."

"There were others?"

"There were three others, his pet yeggs. However, I had a hundred thousand out of him, and after that I lived very well for a couple of years and kept the old place up, and was complimented on my success in the Street!"

He laughed, without grimness, enjoying the memory, as it seemed.

"Only two years? That's fifty thousand a year."

"I mean that I lived well. Gave to the poor, too, like Robin Hood. Poor relations, I should say, to qualify my praise. But they're the hardest kind to give to. They never know what to expect, except a little more than they get."

"At the end of the two years?"

"Then I saw that I'd have to dig in deeper, and this time I chose the Merrill brooch. You've heard of that, I suppose?"

"No, never."

"Merrill was a real-estate broker. He owned an improvement company, and when he got through improving a town, he had all it was worth for the next fifty years mortgaged to the hilt. Then he moved out and improved somewhere else. Mrs. Merrill had the brooch.

"The Merrills didn't splurge in quantity, but they did in quality. He went to India and came back with five rubies, any one of them worth a fortune. It cost him nearly a million, it was said, and I have reason to know that the estimate wasn't extravagant. The big one was in the middle, and the other four set around it. It was big enough to fill the palm of a man's hand, almost, but the silly woman wore it as a brooch!

"One evening we were sitting at dinner, side by side, with a big fireplace just behind us, so I took off the brooch and chucked it back into the ashes.

"After a while, she missed it. There was a great commotion. Everyone was searched, and all that sort of thing. When the search was ended, and every inch of the room had been combed—except the flaming fireplace, of course!—I raked the thing out with the toe of my shoe while I was kindly building up the fire for the sake of the chilly ladies. And I walked home with that million. Of course, I didn't realize fifty per cent, but that was a good deal."

"How long did that last?"

"I increased my scale of living, but still it endured for four years, and would have gone longer, if I hadn't had some bad luck with the ponies."

"Four into five hundred is a hundred and twenty-five a year."

"Yes, I had a good time. The poor relations got less poor. But when the four years ended, I saw that I would have to operate again, and this time I decided that I'd take no chances."

"What sort of chances? In stealing?"

"Not that. I meant to say, I decided to make it safe by stealing so much that I could live on the investment and the interest thereof without having to spend my capital."

"How much did you need for that?"

"I wanted to be moderate—only to maintain the same scale that I had been living on up to that time. I thought that two million would do handsomely. At six percent, there's a hundred and twenty thousand a year, and I thought that that should do."

"Yes," said she, "I should think so!"

"But how was I to make that much money in jewels?"

"Why did you have to stick to jewel robberies?"

"The unfortunate limitation of my mind," said Duval. "Poor David Castle could only do over again what he had already done.

"But he decided that in the first place such a large percentage should not go to the fences. What else to do, then? Why, pearls immediately jumped into my mind. You can take a long string and break it up into units. Not difficult to dispose of them in small quantities anywhere, and at the top market price! So I hunted for rich pearl collectors, and hit upon Henry Hollinshed at once.

"He'd made his money in opium, poor old Henry. Worked hard, handled it from the growth of the poppy to the distribution of the drug in the states, including the smuggling in. His profits were very handsome. He built a church with part of 'em, and endowed a school with another part. But he loved pearls. He was a bachelor, was Henry. He collected the great strings and set pieces for the pleasure of seeing them with his own lonely eyes.

"So I visited Hollinshed, after I'd devoted six months to the serious study of pearls and their values. He kept the pearls in a safe in a corner of his room, a perfectly modern, up-to-date safe, very hard to handle. It was doubly guarded at night, so I went in one noon and blew the door off. It was perfectly simple. I got the collection and disappeared with it through the back cellar door; then I went around in front and watched the police arrive and after them the reporters. I was a plumber, with a plumber's kit—full of pearls, now, besides a few tools—and a smear of lead on my face that would have disguised me from the eyes of the most inquisitive angel.

"Then I went home and on the way knocked my old grip against a lamp-post and spilled out a dozen or more big pearls. Luckily for me they *were* so big, and I gave five cents apiece for them to some boys who were standing near if they would pick up the marbles for me—the ones that had rolled off into corners. I was taking some marbles home to my little boy, you see.

"I thought I had gathered up all of those marbles, but it seems that I hadn't.

"At any rate, I went on home and examined my catch. I wanted to estimate it, but I didn't need to do that. The evening papers said the gross total was nearly three million, and they were only a few hundreds of thousands out of the way.

"I went home, and all was well, but in a few days I had bad news. One of the boys had liked the look of that lustrous marble better than five cents. He kept it; he even showed it to his mother, and by the face of the devil she was a court stenographer's wife who had known better days. She recognized it —thought it was paste—and took it to a jeweller. To a bad one, you'd think—to a cheap, around the corner jeweller, you'd say. Not at all. By the further grace of eminent bad luck she took it to an honest man who nearly fainted and asked her what she was doing with a twenty thousand dollar pearl?

"And immediately there was a hue and cry. The pearl was big enough for Hollinshed to identify it; important enough for him to dig up the record of its sale, exact description of size, weight, color, etc. There was no doubt. It was Hollinshed's pearl. Then who was the greasy, lead-marked young plumber?

"I decided to leave town and disappear entirely. I decided that I'd go where I could rest for a long time, and let the dust settle after this disturbance, for in spite of what the detective story writers say, the police are as clever as fiends, and I dread them to the core of my soul!"

She nodded, her head bent, as it had been for some time.

"And having decided on retirement, what better place than to come West, where I'd spent so many happy summers as a youngster? No sooner said than—"

She raised her head, and Duval heard the merriest of laughter peal beneath the gloom of the trees, flooding them with music as bright as the sun.

"As pretty as a bird atilt on a bough," said Duval, in appreciation. "But why do you laugh?"

"To think of the waste, David! A mere jewel thief, farmer, and man-crusher, when you would have made such a delightful romantic story writer!"

He watched her mirth, still with unchanged appreciation, still with critical thought.

Eventually, he began to laugh in turn.

And she came closer to him, and gasped her admiration, and clasped her hands together at her breast.

"I wish that you'd keep a little farther away, Marian," he told her. "I'm a sedate fellow, a man with a quiet heart, and very much afraid of you, but when you come so close and open your eyes so wide, I grow a little dizzy. You make me feel as though I were standing on a very tall building."

"Do I?" said she.

"You do," said Duval.

She seemed to grow a little puzzled, but at length she snapped her fingers.

"I have it!" she said.

"You have?"

"Yes. You're going to try the other line, now that the first one has failed."

"What other line?"

"You're going to make love to me!"

"Ah," murmured Duval sadly, "you wouldn't believe a word of that either, would you?"

"I *did* believe part of the first one," she confessed. "And so I might believe part of the second. I'd like to try. Will you begin as we walk on?"

"You embarrass me," said Duval. "And you have hold of the arm which I need for gestures.

What's love-making without gestures?"

"But for the sake of love—how I should like to hear you talk then, David!"

"I have quite another way for that," said he.

"Of course you have, and it must be wonderful to hear. What is your other way? I don't presume to guess."

"Oh, very few words. Something manly, direct and simple—the cards all upon the table—here I am—a poor thing, but your own. You see?"

"It wouldn't do out here," said Marian Lane. "We're romantic. We have long evenings without cards, and that lets us read stories, and that makes us want speeches made. If you'll make speeches for me, David, I don't think I can resist."

"I'd need to work them up a bit."

"You could tell me the themes, though."

"You mean eyes and hair, and lips and throat, and all that sort of thing?"

"Well, for a background that would do."

"But I couldn't shine at that, because you know a lot more about your face than I do; I haven't had time to give it the study that you have."

She gave his arm a slight tug that stopped him.

"I like you better and better, David," said she. "If you leave out the face, what *would* you find to want about me?"

"The intriguing devil that makes you torment me, Marian."

"We'd better walk on," said she. "You're growing bad-natured. Is there a devil in me?"

They went on together.

"A mysterious devil, Marian. A cruel, wicked, pain-loving, cunning, prying, eavesdropping devil which would not let poor young Duval alone but took a burning glass and focused it on him, and ever since has kept him writhing and dancing and twisting in the fire until at last he came to you and fell on his knees, as it were, and begged for mercy."

"We'd better turn back," suggested Marian Lane, "because I'm growing uncomfortable."

They swung slowly about and started back.

"Besides," said she, "it really isn't true. I've only shown a perfectly natural, human curiosity."

"Ah, I'm not talking about myself, alone," said Duval. "But there's the rest of the world! All the good fellows about here whose hearts fairly quake when they see Marian Lane, when they speak of Marian Lane, when they so much as think of her gentleness, her industry, her childlike face, her childlike soul. An Iago would melt in the presence of such a girl."

"But not a Duval," said she.

"Why not? He can see that she has spent her days learning to play this neat role, this pretty, guileless part of baby-face that looks up to the big strong men and never changes expression and never lets her mockery get up as far as her eyes, to say nothing of her tongue!"

"But why should I play such a part?" she asked.

"Because if you were yourself, my dear, the acid of your criticism would eat away the sham gold leaf that covers men and let the eyes of the world see their true composition of brass and lead. They would hate you for that. Even if you were more beautiful than you are—though I shouldn't like to try to improve you—men would hate you for knowing the truth about them; for no matter what exquisite care God has showed in forming a woman's flesh, if he puts a brain in the completed picture, men will not endure it. The first thing and the last that we demand of every good woman is that she shall not think. And nothing can save you except one odd chance."

"What's that?"

"Some hundred per cent fellow who will sweep you off your feet, make you as dizzy as you've made others, rattle you away to a church, and marry you before your head clears."

"Here's the end of our walk," she said. "I see the sun through the trees, and I'd better go out alone onto the road."

"I suppose you had, and this is the one friendly time we'll have together. This is the last time, eh?"

"David, David," said she, "I only—"

"Do you have to roll up your eyes like that?" he asked.

"I can't help it," she said. "I've practiced so long that it's deeper than second nature. But I've never wanted to harm you, and I'll never again ask anyone to help me find out who *is* Duval!"

"That's a promise, but I'm afraid you won't keep it."

"So am I," said she.

"Then good-bye, Marian. After this, swords out once more, but now I'm going to say good-bye to everything that's delightful in you."

He took her, deliberately, in his arms.

"Do you mind?" he asked.

"Not at all. I'm delighted," said she, and she turned up her face to him, smiling, and with half-closed eyes.

Duval, however, leaped suddenly back from her. A gun flashed in his hand; then, with a murmur, he made it disappear.

"We've been watched," he told her. "Jude, the sour-faced cur, has trailed us, and I had a glimpse of his eyes as he faded out of sight in the bushes there!"

"That's not the end of the world," she answered.

"That he's seen you in my arms?" cried Duval, strangely excited. "Don't you see? Kinkaid hates me enough without hearing that. And Charlie Nash, when he learns of it—what will even Charlie feel about me? Others, too. It'll be spread through the town in no time. I'm the lucky man, and twenty of them will want to murder me for my good fortune—"

He began to laugh, heartily, but silently.

17

Larry Jude stood in Pete's Place in the late afternoon, when the blacksmith had ended his day of hot labor and stood with elbows on the bar and red, soot-marked face bowed above a tall glass of beer whose thick and creamy collar he had not yet disturbed. Two cowpunchers had just come in, and Tom Main from his ranch with a buckboard loaded with broken harness that needed repair.

When they saw big Larry Jude enter, these men swung half around toward him in dismayed surprise, in disgust, and then instead of speaking fell back to their drinks and looked at one another with faint sneers.

Only Pete himself rose to the occasion.

For Pete was a gentleman to the core of his heart, and he allowed no malice to overcome him.

He asked with a certain amount of solicitude what the big man would have.

"Whisky!"

It was poured, it disappeared.

"Another!"

Pete offered the first general conversation.

"You come from up Montana way, Jude?" asked Pete.

"Naw. But I had a wife up there, once."

"Died?"

"Run away with a half-breed."

He swallowed his third glass of whisky, but refused a fourth.

"The half-breed died sudden," said Larry Jude. He smiled his crooked, evil smile. "I dunno what come of her."

The others could not help a quiet glance at one another. They could guess what had happened to her!

"Lot of women are that way. You never know what way they jump," said Pete, the smoother-over of difficulties. "You see 'em all the time but you can't tell what they'll do. The younger and the prettier they are, the worse trouble maybe they'll make, the more they'll fool everybody. Ain't I right?"

"Take this afternoon," said Jude, "I was out walkin' in the woods, and there I seen the blonde kid from across the street—"

He paused and shook his head with a smile.

An electric shock through the barroom.

"Might you be meanin'," said Pete slowly, picking his words with care and changing color, "might you be meanin' Miss Marian Lane?"

Larry Jude grinned down at his empty glass, turning it methodically between thumb and forefinger.

"What else would I mean?" he burst out suddenly. "She's the girl that nobody can touch, nobody can lay a finger on, she ain't got no steadies. Am I wrong?"

"No, you're right," said Pete. "There ain't a man that's so much as held her hand, and I'm here to say so. There ain't been a word agin her, and there ain't gunna be!"

"Ain't there?" said Jude sourly.

"No, there ain't!" said Pete, and gripped both his fists as he answered the ominous stare of Jude.

"Lemme tell you what I seen," said Jude slowly. "I was out strollin' through the woods, and there I seen this same Marian Lane that makes the boys so dizzy—there I seen her out walkin' with a gent—"

Said Pete, growing hot and white in spots: "I seen her start out. I seen her go up the street, and there wasn't no man with her."

"Sure there wasn't!" said Jude. "Why should there be? Wouldn't it discourage the rest of the boys a lot if they seen her goin' out with one man, day after day? They'd feel a good deal out of place with her, wouldn't they?

"Why should she show herself with a man," continued Jude, "when she can walk up through the woods and find a gent waitin' for her?"

Honest Pete gathered his courage and his strength to burst out. "Jude, mind what you're saying! You're talkin' about a lady, now, man!"

Larry Jude regarded the bartender with a deadly eye.

"Oh, I mind what I'm sayin'," he declared. "I got the facts and the figures, the names and the faces. Would you know what man she'd picked out?

"What man," went on Jude, "is sort of outstandin' from the rest of the herd, here in Moose Creek? What's the man that's made himself taller than the rest of you? Will you tell me that? You know him, well enough. Some of you seen him hypnotize me here in this barroom. You seen him make me take water—"

"Because if it wasn't hypnotism, what was it? Who else ever seen Larry Jude take a back step from any man, and who's ever gunna see it happen again, for one Duval, or for twenty of 'em!"

"I got no better friend in Moose Creek than Duval," said Pete. "There ain't a girl in the world that we all think more of than Marian Lane."

"Don't I know it?" said Jude fiercely. "Ain't that why I'm here? To tell you what fools you all been about her, and about him! Him that hadn't no time for women, eh? Him that couldn't be bothered with 'em, because he was too busy workin'! Why, Duval, I seen him holdin' out his arms to her, and her steppin' into them like a hoss trained to step into its collar."

He broke off with loud laughter, and standing back a little from the bar he glared fiercely around him. Vainly they strove to meet his eyes.

"Why don't they come out into the open?" asked Larry Jude. "Why sneak into the woods and make love? What's on her conscience? Because she still wants the whole town to trail around after her, I reckon. What better idea have you got?"

And, at this point, old Henry himself walked into the saloon for his afternoon glass of beer.

Pete, without a word, served him with his foaming glass.

But Jude turned on the old fellow like a snarling dog.

"Tell Henry, too," said he. "He knows enough already, but I reckon that even Henry don't know about the girl and Duval, their spoonin' in the woods together, their sneakin', lyin' way of livin', and turnin' their backs on each other when they's another person in hearing of 'em! D'you know that, Henry?"

He waited, but Henry, without turning, continued his attention to his beer.

"And tell Duval," went on Larry Jude, "that once he hypnotized me, but the next time, they ain't gunna be time for him to get in his dirty work. I'm waitin' for him to show his face!"

With that, he left the saloon.

Old Henry, having finished his beer, walked without hurry back up the hill and came to Duval's house.

"What's wrong, Henry?" asked Duval. "You look pleased, and that's a sure sign that you're full of bad news!"

"Is it?" asked Henry.

"It is."

"They say that you're philanderin' with Marian Lane, and her with you. The town won't be talkin' nothin' else, by tomorrow, unless you put on the brakes, and keep from rolling downhill."

"Who has told that?" asked Duval, unmoved.

"Why, Larry Jude."

"Jude?"

"Yes."

"Where?"

"In Pete's Place."

"And the boys stood around—all those excellent friends of mine, all those old cronies of Marian Lane, and listened to that talk?"

"It don't cost a thing to use your ears, sir."

"Pete, too?"

"I think Pete tried to stop him, but couldn't. I stayed and gathered up a few seeds of the story after Jude left the place. Only that Jude had seen her in your arms, sir, out in the woods by the creek."

"Is that all? Is that enough to stand Moose Creek on its head?"

"Her being what she is, you being what you are," said Henry, "it'll make considerable commotion, I should say."

"Take the team," said Duval. "I'll be busy for a while. Put up the horse and the mule, and then you'd better wander downtown again and listen to what is being said."

He himself went straight to the corral and saddled the mare.

As he was, with the dust and the sweat of the day's work on him, he buckled a gun belt around his hips, swung into the saddle, and cantered Cherry down to the town.

He went to the store, first of all, and as he dismounted, he saw two old women of Moose Creek go by. They actually turned as though he were a pestilence, and looked bitterly askance at him.

In the store itself there were luckily no customers; only Marian Lane at work behind the counter, tidying up her place and refilling the flour bin with a fresh supply. She greeted him with the pleasantest and most impersonal of smiles.

"I came down," he said, "to find out how everything goes along with you, Marian."

"Perfectly well," she said.

"Our friend Jude has been at Pete's Place telling his little story, it seems!"

"Yes, he has."

"You know about it already?"

"Oh, bad news needs only one jump to go across Moose Creek."

"What's so bad about it, Marian? What sort of a

place is this if a girl's painted black because she—er—"

"Kisses a man?"

"Yes. It was hardly that, you know."

"No. We were interrupted. The secrecy—the woods—and the greatness of Duval, and his contempt for women. All of those things helped to make it worth talking about."

"Did they?"

"Naturally. Best of all, it shows that I'm a hypocrite."

"I don't understand that."

"Yes, I think you do. You explained it pretty fully this afternoon for me."

"I was feeling a bit edgy and said too much."

"You were simply feeling a bit frank, and said what you thought. I don't bear any ill will."

"Will it make any difference to you?"

"To me? Not much."

"But a little?"

"Why, it will cut my business in half, make people talk behind my back, and make the boys sneer in my face. Aside from cheapening me, it doesn't matter a great deal."

He drummed his fingers on the counter. She glanced behind her toward her uncompleted work, as though she were anxious to be back at it, but her proper smile never varied, nor the soft, wide blue of her eyes.

"Marian, you're really eating your heart out about this!"

She looked thoughtfully up at the ceiling, abandoning her smile for the moment.

"No, I don't think I am. At least, I won't for very long. I don't really regret it very much."

"I've come to tell you that I'll do anything you say."

"About what? About Jude and his story?"

"Yes."

"You mean that you'll hunt him down and kill him? Is that why Cherry is standing in the street?"

"Perhaps so."

She shook her head.

"Don't do anything rash, David. Go over to the saloon and tell them that Jude is a puppy, if you wish. But don't, don't use a gun to help out your words!"

"Will you be serious?"

"I am already."

"If you wish, Marian, we'll announce an engagement. We'll let them know that we're going to be married."

"Married? Oh, then they'd be sure that we really had something important to conceal. Even as it is, I'll have to take a few years to live this down."

"You don't think it's a good solution?"

"Marian Lane engaged to whom?"

"To me, of course."

"To David Duval, or to David Castle, or is it really David Smith, or David Jones?"

"You still stick on that point?"

"I'm afraid I do. I still want to know who is Duval."

He stepped back from the counter.

"Oh, but you've done your duty," said the girl. "You've done it beautifully, and I appreciate that!"

He bowed to her, and went slowly out of the store.

Duval looked up and down the way gloomily.

The peace which had been here in Moose Creek like a gold mine for him had now disappeared.

But he crossed the street to Pete's Place and went in to find only Tom Main and Pete himself present.

By the guilty manner in which they glanced up and then straightened, Duval could guess what had been the subject of their conversation.

He felt also, and instantly, that there was very little use in trying words, so he merely leaned against the bar and took a small whisky with the two. It was Tom Main who treated.

"Jude has been down here with some ugly talk," said Duval. "Is that correct?"

Pete nodded uneasily.

"I'm not angry, except for Marian Lane," said Duval.

"Sure," said Pete, and bit his lip in anxiety.

It was plain that he wanted to believe whatever Duval would say; it was also plain that he would have a hard time doing so.

"If Jude comes along again," said Duval, "I'd like to see him. My old man used to say there was no way to stop a grass fire except backfiring agin it. If he should drop in and you'd send me word, Pete, I'd take it mighty kindly!"

"Why—sure," said Pete. "I'd do that, only I reckon that Jude won't be comin' in again. He's done his job!"

Silence fell heavily over the old barroom and finally Duval left.

At the door he paused again, looking back toward the others, and they, anxiously, toward him.

"Look here, boys," said he. "Because I was fool enough to try to kiss Marian Lane, and because my friend Larry Jude says I *did* kiss her, is there any reason why he's to be believed above me? If there is, say so!"

They both waved deprecatory hands.

"There ain't any reason in the world, Duval!" Main assured him. "Jude's a skunk and he's got it in for you. Nobody'll pay no attention to him."

But the words rang flat as a counterfeit coin, and Duval knew that he had lost this trick in the game as he went out onto the street again.

Ordinarily, it would have been of no importance, for it was only a bit of gossip and that of the lightest kind; and yet he knew that his position in Moose Creek was imperilled. His strength there had been the friendship of the men of the town and the community around it. That friendship was now endangered, and as he rode back up the hill Duval made up his mind definitely to leave Moose Creek and start for another region.

18

When Jude left the saloon, he did not tarry, he knew that imminent danger was close at his heels, and therefore he went with rapidity straight for the place where he knew he would find Kinkaid. This was back among the hills at a small shanty, long deserted and staggering now to the ground. And he found Kinkaid seated inside on a sagging box, his back against the wall and his arms folded across his chest.

There was no greeting between them. Each was equally distasteful to the other, and through the darkening of the day they looked gloomily at one another.

"Duval is on the skids," said Jude, beginning abruptly.

"Duval?" growled the marshal, as though the name were new to him.

"It works out like a card trick," said Jude.

He leaned against the side of the door and, as one who has done good work and can afford to relax, he rolled a cigarette, lighted it, inhaled deeply.

"It was kind of hard to get at him; he had too many friends; it ain't hard now!"

"Go on," said Kinkaid as gruffly as before.

"They liked Duval. Most of those young gents liked something else a little better."

"What was that?"

"The grocery store girl—Marian Lane. She's all they could see at one look!"

"Jude," said the marshal, "we're workin' together on one job—Duval. Other folks don't count. We'll leave out the girl, for a beginning, I reckon!"

"You can't leave her out, because she's in the town and in the game of Duval."

"She is? Talk straight, and talk slow, Jude!"

The latter shrugged his shoulders at the warning in the tone of Kinkaid.

"Suppose," went on Jude, "that a gent rolled into Moose Creek and mopped up all the attention of Marian Lane. Would the other young gents have much use for him? Would he be popular, I mean, around the town and along the range?"

Kinkaid leaned forward, then settled back again.

"Has—Duval done that?" he asked briefly.

But there was a change in his voice, and Jude grinned with sour delight.

"I trailed him as I said I would. I watched him all day, and it wasn't no easy job. He was harrowin', but every time there was a stir of the bushes in the wind, he'd whirl around and have a look at it, and his gun is only a hundredth part of a second behind his look, if he means business!"

"Go on!" said the marshal wearily. "Tell how brave you were, lyin' on the ground on your belly and watchin' Duval. Want me to praise you for that, Jude?"

Jude shrugged his shoulders.

"What you think ain't of no importance to me,

but if you ain't watched that cat, you might take a few minutes off some day and have a look at him! He's worth while."

"Thanks, I know enough about him. Go on, Jude," Kinkaid ordered calmly.

"Anyway I trailed him like his shadow, and in the afternoon, I seen him meet Marian Lane in the woods."

There was a brief exclamation from the marshal. "Where?"

"Along the creek. He went over and sat down on a stone. Pretty soon she came along and met him."

"What did they do?"

"Talked—and walked along."

"When they met?"

"Nothin' but talk. I was too far away to get hold of that, mostly, and what I did hear was kind of hard to understand. But I found out one thing."

"Go on. You take a year to say nothing!"

"You'll think it's something. The lingo that he slings around as if he was fresh off the range ain't his natural lingo at all!"

"What's the proof of that?"

"He talked like a book to the girl!"

"What did he say?"

"I don't remember, except that no schoolteacher could of talked closer to a book."

"Good!" said the marshal slowly. "I thought that he—but I didn't figger on this—"

He controlled himself, but Jude went on: "You thought he was a crook. You hoped that he was a crook. But you didn't guess how big a crook he was! Well, he's that kind. Can use both sides of his tongue as fair as any man in the world! I listened to the talk as much as I could."

"Where did they go?"

"Up the creek a way, and then they turned around and they come back together."

"What's there in that?"

"When they quit each other, they didn't go out onto the road. They said good-bye under the trees, where the shadows was pretty thick over 'em!"

"Yes?" queried the marshal with a rising emotion.

"Duval, he steps up and holds out his arms, and she walked right into 'em as if they was home for her—"

The marshal was suddenly erect, and striding to Jude, he gripped him by both arms, and forced him back into the open where, by the last of the daylight, he could dimly read the other's face.

"Jude, if you're lyin' to me," he said, "I'll have your hide off of you for saddle leather!"

"Leave go your hold of me," said Jude in angry answer. "I'll not be manhandled by no lousy marshal, even if his name is Kinkaid! Leave go your hands from me, d'you hear?"

The marshal obeyed, because already he was sure of the man's truth in this recital.

"She steps into his arms, and he folds her up in 'em, like a storekeeper wrappin' up a Christmas toy. He folds her up in 'em and leans over and what does she do?"

"Get done with this, will you?" demanded Kinkaid, his voice harsh with anger.

"Ay, it don't please you none, I can see," said Jude, the expert in pain-giving. "It don't please you none, and it didn't much more please me, neither. But I see when he leaned over her, that she lifted up her face for him to kiss—"

"Hell and fire!" burst out Kinkaid. "The sneakin', hypocritical, wo'thless woman!"

Jude broke into a jeering laughter.

"That puts the whip on the raw, I reckon," he said. "That'll make you pull a load uphill, eh? Well, I seen what it would do, and when I found out—"

"What did you do?"

"Went to Pete's Place, because it was the same as goin' to a newspaper. Went to Pete's Place and I told 'em what I seen!"

"*You* went back to Pete's Place?"

Jude drew in his breath through his teeth with an audible whistle.

"I went back there, where he made a cur out of me, where he busted me down almost to cryin'— where he kicked me out onto the street! I went back there and I faced the boys in Pete's. I told 'em what I'd seen.

"They took it hard," added Jude, "though most of 'em hung onto themselves better than you done. But they were all galled by it a little bit, I can tell you. It hurt. It hurt 'em bad!"

"What did they do?"

"Nothin'. What could they do? But now every man jack of 'em figgers that Duval has got what they all wanted. Henry come in for a part of the yarn. I talked to his face, and I told him that I wanted to meet Duval agin!"

"You lied!"

"Maybe I did," answered the other with a strange frankness. "Maybe once havin' felt his eye, I wouldn't be no good no more agin him. But I gotta hope, don't I? I gotta hope that some day I can have a chance back at him, and then get him, or else he gets me, and I die like a man, and not like no damn coward!"

"What happened then?"

"As I started out, I went up the road behind the brush, and I seen Duval come slidin' down the hill on the mare, Cherry. He was aimed at makin' trouble. I guess that Henry had gone back and told him!"

"Then Henry's alone at the cabin?"

"He is, unless Duval has come straight back from the town."

"He ain't goin' straight back," declared Kinkaid. "He's gunna wait down there in the town, and try what his talk can do to rub out what you told 'em!"

"He won't have no success at all," said Jude. "You can mistake a lie for the truth but not after truth has been along and showed its real face at you!"

"Wait!" muttered the marshal. "Duval gone—only Henry in the house—what's a better chance than that to get inside the house, I'd like to know."

"You mean to go inside of Duval's house? Why not go and put your foot in a steel bear-trap?" asked Jude, angrily, and yet touched with admiration. "You'll be tellin' me pretty soon that you got no fear of any man in the world!"

"I mean it," answered the marshal firmly. "But now let's go down and get to Duval's place. He may be started back now."

It was not pleasant to Jude to go to Duval's house. Having faced Duval once, he would, as he expressed it well, as soon have put his foot inside a steel bear-trap. However, since the marshal would have it so, so it must be!

So they came to the verge of Duval's place and dismounted.

The marshal was not particularly sensitive to the feelings of others, but he could sense Jude's cold dread and he remarked shortly: "Stay here, then. And—if they's a sight of Duval comin' back up the road, or a sound of his hoss—you could tell the long beat of her gallop, I reckon—you whistle to me, not too loud, and I'll—know what to expect."

"Suppose he's there now?"

Kinkaid peered through the hedge.

"The house ain't lighted," he argued. "If he was there, they'd be a light—maybe—"

He left his sentence unfinished, as the possibilities of disaster surged up into his mind.

Yet the marshal's spirit, unlike Jude's, had not been broken. He hesitated only one moment, and then slid through the shrubbery and stalked with long strides straight for the cabin.

He did not attempt to stalk the place. He marched straight to the door and beat against it.

He heard the hollow echo of the knock die swiftly inside, so thrust the door wide and entered.

Unshuttering the dark lantern which he carried he started to work.

He found the trap which led to the cellar, opened it, and descended into the moist coolness of the lower house.

The walls were roughly masoned stone; the floor was merely packed dirt; and first he went around the walls, tapping them cautiously, and listening to find the hollow sound which would mean a cavity within. It was difficult work, but it was work in which the marshal was an expert.

It was while he proceeded in this fashion that he

stepped on what seemed to him a softer portion of the floor, and turning the full light of the lantern upon it, he was reasonably sure that here the earth was actually a shade more loose, and that it was heaped a trifle above the surrounding level.

Instantly he was scooping it away; in a moment he had touched oiled silk; in another instant there was spread out on the cellar floor a gleaming row of burglar's tools, of the finest steel, of the latest fashion. He regarded them with an appreciative eye but he did not take them.

Instead, he rolled them up exactly as they had been, and replacing them in the hole, he cautiously restored the earth, and spent a moment stamping down the soil which he had displaced.

Here it occurred to Kinkaid that any warning whistle would hardly reach him as he worked in the cellar; moreover, had he not found enough?

He hastened up the ladder to the house itself and went to the door. But here he paused, uncertain, ill at ease.

Gritting his teeth he turned back to the cellar door. Here, with his hand upon it, the perspiration rolled out on his forehead and beneath the pits of his arms.

Whatever else he did, he could not return to the cellar below, so far from freedom, and telling himself that, after all, that cellar would yield him no more returns, he gave himself to the search of the house itself. He would take the attic later. In the meantime, here were the walls and the floor of the house.

So the ray of the lantern began to pass around the walls, scrutinizing every joint of the logs until Kinkaid came to the short angling logs which built up one blunt corner. To tap the logs here, he had to reach across the bed.

The very first stroke he made rang hollow on his ear!

He had to pause to wipe his face, because the sweat was blinding him, but then he started a serious examination of that log. Those above and below it were normal to the ear, but this one was distinctly flawed. At last, gripping it with both hands, he jerked back—and the front face of it came easily away!

Within, he found two things.

The first was to him beyond all price, for it was the gun belt which he had lost, the brown-rubbed holster, and within the holster his own revolver with the nine storied notches in its handle.

He dragged it out with the joy of an Indian recovering his medicine bag.

There remained the second object in this homemade niche.

It was a small chamois sack, the mouth of which he pulled wide and poured some of the contents into his hand. He blinked at what he found, jerking the string which closed the sack, and dropped it into his pocket.

He had found all that he wished, a thousand times more. He held Duval in the cup of his hand, as it were; and yet there was nothing to be gained and much to be lost by letting Duval know at once that he was destroyed!

So he picked up the section of log which he had removed and replaced it. It was while he was pushing it home that Kinkaid heard the whistle, and hearing it, knew that the same sound had been in his ear before.

He stood back, therefore, against the wall, as he heard the approaching footfall, and drawing his own revolver, his tried and proved weapon, he gripped it hard, until the notches rubbed into his skin. At that distance, he would not fail!

So he raised it, levelled it, and as a footstep approached the cabin from without, he prepared to shoot Duval the instant his silhouette appeared dimly embraced within the rectangle of the door, against the stars of the horizon.

A weary voice sounded—"I thought I'd closed this door when I left—I'm getting old!"

The voice of Henry!

In mid-impulse against the trigger, Kinkaid checked his forefinger. And standing at ease, smiling now, he waited until old Henry had lighted a lamp, blown out the match, and was standing back from the growing flame in the chimney of the lamp.

Then he said: "Henry, don't turn 'round!"

Henry jerked halfway about in spite of that command; then controlled the motion.

"Well, well," said he, "if it ain't the marshal come back to pay a sort of a surprise call on us!"

"I've come to pay a call," said the marshal grimly. "And I was sorry to find you both out of the place. Where's your boss?"

"Him? Oh, he's gone off on the mare."

"You lie!"

"Look in the corral, then."

"Where did he go?"

"Where you'll never find him, if he don't want to be found!"

Kinkaid could not keep back the curse that leaped to his lips at this unwelcome news.

"Gone?"

"I dunno," said old Henry. "I never know what he'll do. But whatever it is, I know that it'll be too deep and hard for you to follow, Kinkaid!"

The marshal laughed.

"You poor trustin' fool!" said he. "You jackass! I got Duval in the palm of my hand. March out the door."

"Me? What's wrong with me?"

"Robbery's what's wrong with you, man!"

"Robbery? There's an idea!" said old Henry.

But, as he spoke, his hand glided beneath his coat. For some reason, the instant that movement began, Kinkaid knew what it meant. He did not fear for himself, but understood Henry's intention was to take his own life.

So he leaped wonderfully swiftly for a man of his size, and as the muzzle of the weapon whipped up under Henry's chin, Kinkaid struck the hand away. The next instant the report of the gun thundered in the room.

The noise of the revolver exploding made Kinkaid hasten his prisoner, unharmed, into the open, merely pausing to kick the door to with a thrust of his heel, and while he did so he heard a guarded whistle from the hedge.

"That's the signal, eh?" said Henry musingly. "That's the warning for you, Kinkaid, when you come robbing?"

The marshal threw a fold of his big bandanna over the mouth of his captive and held it tight twisted at the nape of his neck. In that manner he effectually silenced old Henry, and with his free hand gripping the old man by the elbow, he forced him rapidly forward toward the hedge.

But in the meantime, up from the lower gate

came the swinging beat of the hoofs of a horse, and as though sunshine fell upon her, Kinkaid thought he could see the striding of the mare, Cherry.

He hurried his prisoner on, therefore, until they came to the hedge. There he paused, fearing to call Duval's attention by making any sound of rustling in passing through.

Duval, in the meantime, had reached the corral and was inside it, unsaddling the mare.

"Henry!" he called. "Henry!" he called again.

Then big Kinkaid distinctly heard the other murmur: "The old fellow's losing his ears."

Shortly afterward the whistle of Duval went toward the house, and as the sound grew dim around the corner of the cabin, Kinkaid plunged through the hedge and gained the road beyond.

"One for me!" he said briefly to the waiting Jude.

A strangled voice began in Jude's throat and dissolved into the words: "Was that—was that whistle Duval? I thought that was the gallop of the mare!"

"Gimme your hoss," said Kinkaid in answer.

And as the other let it up, Kinkaid with his gigantic strength lifted old Henry and literally threw him into the saddle. He mounted his own horse the next instant and rode on at a slow walk, lest the beat of hoofs convey some message to Duval.

But no horseman appeared, while they passed slowly down byways to the rear of the town, and so to the back door of Sheriff Nat Adare's sanctum, the Moose Creek jail.

It was opened at the marshal's knock.

"Who's there?" asked the jailer, growling out through a crack of the door.

The marshal's heavy hand cast the door wide open and nearly felled the jailer.

"Kinkaid and a prisoner!" he announced. "Open up for me and show me the cells!"

Into the central one of these, Kinkaid had the prisoner locked.

"Got food?" he asked.

"Rice and molasses," said the latter. "I'll go get—"

"That's good enough for him," declared Kinkaid. "Feed him. Jude, come with me!"

He went out to the rear of the jail again, and there talked quietly with Jude in the darkness.

"And—him?" said Jude in a shaken voice, gesturing with his thumb over his shoulder. "Duval? Is he gunna go loose?"

"He's got to go loose for a while," said the marshal. "I've got enough to get him—but I can't spring it for a while. I've got to get a little extra proof, and then I'll close in on him. But in the meantime, he's gunna find out what I've done. He'll find out before morning where Henry is. He may find out before that what I've taken from the house."

"And run?"

"I dunno," said the marshal thoughtfully. "I guess he won't run or leastways very far. By the way I write him down, he ain't the kind that'll run out on a partner, and Henry's a friend of his. He'll stand by to try to help Henry. And Henry's the bait that'll be dangled in front of him until I've got the proof that I need and can put the irons on him! If I could of left the stuff there—if I could of left the stuff there—"

He paused, with a wistful note in his voice, then

concluded: "That would of made it easy to get all the proofs I need, I reckon. But I couldn't do that! What I want you to do is to go back up there and shadow the house!"

"Me?"

"Yes, you."

"I can't do it," said the other with calm decision. "I ain't got the nerve to do it—yet! Maybe I'll get it later on and try. But just now, I'm played out!"

The marshal hesitated, breathing hard, he was so angered by this weakness; yet he said not a word of reproof. He merely laid a comforting hand upon the shoulder of his companion and murmured: "Stay a while and steady up, man! You'll be all right again. Everybody gets the jumps at this game. If you find that you can get up there later and use your ears and your eyes, I'd take it kind!"

Inside the jail, he went at once to Henry, who was finishing his plate of rice and molasses with proper philosophic unconcern. The marshal remained outside the bars and suddenly thrust through them the chamois bag.

"Ever see this, Henry?"

Henry looked with an impatient frown.

"No," said he.

And the marshal believed him; in part, because he wished to believe.

"Henry," said he, "I guess you know how you'll get off with an easy sentence?"

"I dunno nothing," said Henry pleasantly.

He shaded his eyes, the better to see the face of the marshal.

"You know, but I'll tell you, anyway. Tell me where to get the stuff you took from Broom and Carson's safe!"

"Broom and Carson's safe? Are you saddlin' that on me?"

He chuckled a little, and wagged his head at Kinkaid.

"You've still got the bandage on your finger, man," said Kinkaid. "It's the pen for you, anyway. The only thing is that if we get the money back, on account of you being old and all, the judge might parole you. Anyway, he wouldn't make it a heavy sentence. I'd answer for that!"

"You'd answer, would you?" said the old man calmly. "You double-crossing sneak!"

Kinkaid started.

"You think I wouldn't keep my end of the bargain, Henry?"

"Damn you and all your bloodhound kind," said Henry without special emphasis. "I'll take my chances outside of your promises."

"It's a clear case, Henry," said the marshal with much patience. "The prints of the mare's shoes, and the wound on your hand. How can you dodge that? D'you count on Duval to get you out of this?"

"Why not?"

Kinkaid knocked against the bars. "Tool-proof steel!" said he. "I reckon that's enough of an answer for you, my son!"

However, Henry chuckled and shook his head.

"You got a wise head on your shoulders," said he. "You know a lot, Kinkaid, but you don't know much about Duval. You've had him with his back to the wall once, and he slipped out and was behind you before you could hit him once. And that'll happen again, and again! You could have Duval cornered twenty times, Kinkaid, and every time he'd show you how much better he was than you even dreamed that he could be."

"Is he gunna kill me?" asked the marshal, half contemptuous and half curious.

"He's gunna kill you, Kinkaid," said Henry soberly, "as sure as I'm sittin' here in jail. Lay your money on it, and make out your will."

"Henry," said the marshal, "I pretty nigh like you, when I hear you talk like this, but lemme tell you that the next time I meet Duval, it'll be face to face, and then God help him. He'll go where nine have gone before him! But about you—they's one *sure* way you can get out of jail—maybe even without turnin' in *all* of the money that you got from Broom and Carson, and that's to tell me who is Duval?"

19

Kinkaid waited a moment for Henry to speak, but the old man was lost in thought.

"Suppose," said the marshal, "that everything was returned to Broom and Carson except fifty thousand dollars—that could be put down to commission, say. For the rest of that money, they'd be willing not to press the charges home. You see?"

Henry nodded.

"That would be fifty thousand for me," said he. "Fifty thousand clear, and Duval—where?"

"Wherever you could put him. You know where that would be a tolerable lot better than I do! In the pen; up Salt Creek. I dunno, but you ought to know!"

Old Henry's eyes turned positively green; but in the very crisis of temptation, he suddenly shrugged his shoulders and cast out his hands in a gesture of dismissal.

"You won't do it?" asked the marshal.

"There ain't a thing against Duval," said Henry.

"That's a lie! I seen it in your eyes!"

"I was trying to work up a lie," said Henry steadily, "but I seen it was no use trying. There ain't a thing against him!"

"Why, you fool," said the marshal, "you'll get life out of this—twenty years, anyway. You'll die in stripes!"

"Stripes ain't on the skin; they're only on the clothes," said Henry. "And they got long sleepin' hours, besides, in a good up-to-date pen."

"Listen to me!" urged Kinkaid. "There's no chance that Duval could harm you. Tell me what I want to know, and I'll have him gathered up in one day and put away in irons!"

"Put irons on a ghost!" answered Henry. "You talk—well the way I'd expect you to talk!"

Then he added, while Kinkaid strove to find another argument: "Suppose that I had something over his head, what'd he do? Either get me safe out if he thought I'd play straight, or else slip in and shoot me through the head if he thought I wouldn't. Don't talk to me, man. I *know* Duval. You only do a little guessing about him!"

"Then I'll make you this promise," said the marshal fiercely. "If they was a hundred hands on Duval, none of 'em will ever open the door of this cell. If they do, may I die!"

He turned and walked away with great strides, and found the sheriff just entering the jail. Old Nat Adare looked still full of sleep but he blinked himself nearer awake when he saw the other before him.

Kinkaid was too irritated to be diplomatic. He laid his immense hand on the shoulder of the sheriff and said: "Adare, I've put an old man in that cell yonder. He ain't gunna do much himself, though he's a lot smarter than you may think. But on the outside, I got an idea the smartest man that ever come over the mountains is gunna try to free him. Can you keep him safe?"

"Extra guards—"

"Extra guards can be bought up," said the marshal. "If you can hire 'em, somebody else can pay a higher price. Ain't that right?"

"I'll be here myself," said Adare. "Who's the outside man?"

"I dunno. I'm tryin' to find out!" said the marshal, and abruptly left.

In spite of his bluffness, he felt a great deal of trust in the honesty and the alertness of the sheriff; he knew the veteran would be on his mettle after the challenge which had been delivered, and he felt that odds were nine out of ten in favor of keeping his prisoner securely.

In the meantime, he had other preparations to make.

Mr. Broom of Broom and Carson was a man of adroit mind and swift as any ferret in his thoughts. He looked like a ferret, in fact. That is to say, he was a little man with a long neck, and a very small head. He looked almost as though he could button his collar and then put it on over his head. His ways were as swift as his thoughts, moreover, and he could rarely stay still for a moment. When he sat down, he was continually twisting from side to side, shifting his feet, jerking his head back and forth, interlacing and then separating his fingers.

In his own room, the first problem that he put to himself was: In what manner can I shift the total loss to the shoulders of my partner?

For Carson, bigger and slower than Broom, was infinitely more stupid just as he was infinitely more honest.

Their partnership had been based upon Carson's money and Broom's brains. Mr. Carson wanted to be rich, but he wanted to be honest. Mr. Brown wanted to be rich and thought that any means were justified that led to the golden end.

In the beginning he had been the obsequious servant of his wealthier partner. But now Carson was in a minority.

Yet, no matter how he turned the matter back and forth through his mind, Broom was unable to find a way of taking all the loss out of Carson's pocket. His failure to come to this desired end drove him almost mad, and it was while his nerves were jumping at their worst that his wife tapped on the door.

"Well!" screamed Broom, and since one word rarely did for him, he kept on shrieking: "Well? Well? Well?" several times. It helped him a little to speak in this manner.

"There's a man to see you," said his wife timidly through the door.

"Damn the man that wants to see me!" yelled Mr. Broom. "Damn you—damn everything! You wanta drive me crazy!"

He smashed at the door with his fist to emphasize his point.

Mrs. Broom, who seemed to have guessed what would happen in response to her knock and her words, already had shrunk back across the hall, so that Mr. Broom saw, directly in front of him, just inside the front door, the man who had come to see him. He was most rudely dressed in blue jeans that bagged enormously at the knees; he had on no coat, but only a loose blue-flannel shirt, and he carried his slouch hat in his hand.

"You wanta see me! You wanta see me! You wanta job, I guess? You come beggin' for a job—this time of night—takin' my time—no, I won't take you—damn you, you fool—get out! I wouldn't have you—not for a gift—you—"

He stopped his speech and his advance at the same moment, not because he had exhausted either his vocabulary or his vindictiveness, but because he was stopped by a short, shrill cry from his wife who ran suddenly in front of him and caught his arms. "Archie! Archie! *Archie!* " she implored. "It's Duval!"

"God bless me!" said Mr. Archie Broom. "Duval! Duval!—Bad light—blockheads always coming around for a job—day and night—no peace—no rest—always harassed—terrible mistake—glad to see you, Duval. Terribly glad to see you. Come right in! What can I do for you? What will you have? Heard so much—simply delighted—this is my wife—come this way—"

He led Duval into his office, and when the latter was seated, Mr. Broom himself fell into a chair, exhausted for the moment by fear.

"Now, Mr. Duval," said the lumberman, "what is there that I can do for you?"

He rubbed his hands together.

"Honor to have you here, sir. We've heard a lot—Moose Creek talks about people, you know? But the man who's with you—that Henry—that scoundrel—I beg your pardon—probably a mistake—but said to have been the one who robbed me! Who robbed me—almost a quarter of a million! I beg your pardon. No offense to you, Mr. Duval. Wouldn't offend you! Let's forget Henry. What can I do for you, sir?"

Duval listened to this rapid, broken outpouring of words without impatience, and then answered: "I don't know of anything that you can do for me. But I dropped in here sort of thinkin' that I might be able to do something for you, Mr. Broom."

The latter tapped himself rapidly upon the breastbone.

"You for me? You for me?" he said, delighted and amazed. "What could you do for me, then?"

"I don't know if we could make a bargain," said Duval. "But it seems to me a mighty shame that old Henry should be in jail—and that you should be out all that money. Don't that sound as though we could meet, somehow?"

Broom grinned, agape, at Duval, like a thirst-starved man at a vision of blue, cool water.

"A hundred and eighty thousand dollars! Duval, Duval, you've brought it along with you! Don't say a word! Just bring it in to me. That's all. Not a word! Just bring in the money. I'll dismiss the charges against Henry. I'll—have a cigar, Mr. Duval. Honor to have you here with me. Delighted—no idea how much we've talked—everybody talked—here's a match—don't smoke cigars? But where's the money, Duval? Where's the money?"

"Well," said Duval, "I reckon the money's safe. My old man used to say that money that was put away wasn't likely to go off and spend itself!"

Although Broom wore his collars large, he now freed the one he had on to make his breathing easier.

"None of it, Duval?" he said. "None of it spent? None of it split up and gone? Still the whole wad altogether?"

"Not a penny gone," said Duval quietly.

Broom relaxed in the chair, fell back into it, disjoined his hands, which fell loosely into his lap, and exhaled a long breath.

"Well, then, let's have it out! Let's have it out! Let's have it out!" he chattered. "I'll be glad to see it all again. Not that I'll forget you, Duval! You'll come in for a commission. Something handsome! That's a mere detail. Settle that later on, eh? But to get the money here—probably outside in your saddlebags, Duval?"

He gaped with a sort of horrible expectancy.

Duval replied: "You get the money back without a commission subtracted. But what about Henry?"

"I drop all charges—"

"Does that mean that Kinkaid will drop all charges, as well?"

"Kinkaid? Kinkaid? Why, all the marshal wants to do is to get my money back for me."

"Kinkaid? Money? Is Kinkaid any friend of yours?"

Broom wrung his hands in nervous indecision.

"Kinkaid? Friend? Kinkaid is—is—"

"Aimed tolerable straight at jailin' of a crook. He's got the right man, it looks like!"

"You admit that Henry did it, of course?"

"Sure I admit it. The marshal has the proofs, too. Only, Henry ought to—"

"No matter what happens to Henry, you, as an honest man—your duty to society—your duty to me—a fellow man—must give up the money, no matter what happens to Henry! You agree to that? Of course you agree. Can see fine integrity in your face, Duval—I—I—"

"The marshal never would give away a trick,"

answered Duval flatly. "He ain't got that reputation. He loves a jailed crook because he's jailed, and that's the only reason! But you don't get a penny until Henry's free, outside of that jail!"

"Meaning what? Meaning what?"

"Meaning that no matter what sort of a charge is over his head, if you'll get Henry out of that jail, I'll give you back your money!"

"Mr. Duval!" gasped Broom. "But suppose that after Henry's delivered something happened—something that made you change your mind about paying back—"

Duval smiled.

"That's a chance you gotta take, Broom. You got my word for it. If you wanta gamble on that, all right. If you don't, I'll step along my way!"

Mr. Broom twisted violently two or three times in his chair, from one side of it to the other.

"Dear me! Dear me! Dear me!" he repeated rapidly. "I'll have to have a little time. I'll have to think—I'll have to see my partner."

"There ain't time for that," replied Duval. "Henry comes out of that jail tonight, or the deal's off!"

"What?" screamed Broom.

He suddenly leaped from his chair and shrieked: "You come here pretending to be an honest man and you—"

He remembered himself, the recovery shocking him back almost prostrate in his chair again.

"Duval," he said tremulously, when he had recovered some measure of his self-composure, "I didn't mean that. I'll do what I can—but a jail—a guarded jail—Kinkaid—oh, my God! My God!"

He began to wring his hands.

But, even in this dilemma, his keen eyes jerked from side to side as he searched for a new expedient.

"You!" he shouted suddenly. "You could do it, Duval! You could do anything. They all say so! You can get him out!"

"They ain't nothin' they're watchin' for so close, there around the jail, as Duval. I can't do a thing for Henry. It's up to you, Mr. Broom."

Broom, in despair, threw both arms stiffly above his head and kept them there, the hands trembling violently in his excess of emotion.

"What can I do?" he asked.

"You can go to see Henry. They'll let you see him."

"And then what?"

"Suppose that I could find a way for you to turn him loose—you'd have to show your nerve, Broom. Have you got it on tap tonight?"

Mr. Broom laughed through his teeth.

"I've got a hundred and eighty thousand dollars' worth of nerve," said he. "Is that enough? I've got all of that."

"I get you," answered Duval, "and it sounds tolerable fine, to me. There ought to be just about enough nerve in that to get you through and land Henry out of jail. And then you could collect what you've invested, Broom. Is it a go?"

The other stretched out his hand and Duval, after an instant of hesitation, accepted it.

20

For not more than a quarter of an hour, Duval was in Broom's house, talking rapidly, earnestly with the little man.

Then he left, mounted the waiting mare, and galloped rapidly back to his own shack.

He did not approach it with any caution, though he was fairly sure that the little house was being watched by some agent of the marshal, but instead, he galloped through the open gate and straight up to his door.

There he dismounted, and passed inside the cabin, lighted the lamp, and with it examined the room with a sweeping glance. As though making up his mind that nothing remained of any significance except in one place, he went to his row of books and opened several of them in rapid succession, taking out a few papers that had been lodged among the pages of each.

That done, he went to the corner logs, removed the false half which the marshal already had taken out, and looked with a nod of understanding into the cavity.

He replaced the covering wood, and now fastened over his left shoulder a strap that was reinforced by another girded loosely around his breast. Under his armpit, depending from the first strap, he secured a strong clip, and into this he passed the long Colt revolver. Then, picking up a big, loosely fitting coat, he shrugged it over his shoulders.

Wearing it open in front, he walked a few times up and down the room, practicing the draw.

When all was at last in readiness to please him, he extinguished the lamp, and standing at his door for a moment, he listened with ear canted down, to every small sound that stirred among the trees, whether of the leaves rustling in the wind, or the boughs softly moaning as they rubbed one another.

He seemed at last content, so went on back to the horse shed, where he saddled that same animal on which he had first ridden into Moose Creek. This horse he led back to the cabin, from which he carried out matches, bacon, coffee, sugar, salt, and flour, some baking powder and some raisins, and loaded all these provisions into the saddlebags together with a couple of cooking utensils. Behind the saddle he tied a roll of blankets, wrapped in a big slicker. Into the saddle holster he thrust the long barrel of a Winchester repeating rifle, and over the horn of the saddle he suspended a loaded cartridge belt.

Then he rode through the gate, turned, and closed it behind him.

He did not, however, turn away from the town but directly toward it, and skirting toward the rear of the village, very much as the marshal had done not so long before him, he came to the back of the jail where Henry was a prisoner.

Here he halted, dismounted where the shrubbery stood thick and high as a horse's head, and threw the reins of both animals. Just before him was the office of the jail, and as he stood there a light flickered dimly behind them, as though a match were being lighted; then the illumination waned, steadied, and grew until full lamplight was flooding both the apertures.

Inside, at that moment, the sheriff was saying to Mr. Broom, of Broom and Carson: "You set yourself here and wait a while. I don't like to do it, though, because this here is the marshal's prisoner, and if anything happened to him, I'd never hear the last of it."

"Look here, look here!" snapped Broom. "Am I likely to let the man go free? Answer me that? Am I likely to set him free?"

"It ain't likelihoods," said the sheriff, "that I'm talkin' about. It's the possibilities."

"Is it possible, then?" shouted Broom. "Tell me that, Sheriff Adare! Is it possible? How could I turn him loose?"

"Well, I dunno," said Adare frankly, "and if I did, no matter how much I thought of you, Mr. Broom, I wouldn't let him come in here and stay alone with you!"

"Of course you wouldn't," said Broom. "That's only natural. But as it is—"

"I dunno that I can do it, anyway," said the other. "Fact is, Mr. Broom, the marshal expects to learn somethin' out of that man, and Henry's promised that if he ain't free before tomorrow noon, he's gunna open up and talk and say some things that the marshal is a pile more interested in than he is in Henry himself and your lost money, too!"

"More than a hundred and eighty thousand

dollars?" exclaimed the other. "Mind that, sheriff! Things come to a pretty pass when a Federal officer lets a hundred and eighty thousand dollars slide for the sake of what a scoundrel can tell him —about what?"

"Ay, Mr. Broom, there you are! I ain't one of the deep ones and I dunno. But Dick Kinkaid, he *is* deep. He's clean over my head, and I dunno what he's drivin' at. But he's mighty smart and he ain't often wrong in the last count of things. You gotta say that for him, eh?"

"Perhaps, perhaps!" said Mr. Broom. "However, let's have your friend Henry in here."

"You think you can do something with him, eh?"

"I think that I can."

"But still—it ain't likely that you could persuade him, when Kinkaid himself has such a hard time about it!"

Mr. Broom's face glistened in a sudden sweat of anxiety, and starting up from his chair, he pointed dramatically out of the nearest window.

"Listen, will you?"

"Ay, and what is it?" demanded the sheriff, cocking his ear.

"Rain, rain, rain, rain!" burst out Broom.

Nat Adare, blinking at him, shook his head, unable to make a connection between his violent speech and the preceding conversation.

"Rain, rain!" yelled Broom, "and likely the money is lying out. A hundred and eighty thousand dollars that's washing and rotting away, because you won't let me have a word with your prisoner—"

"Hold on, hold on!" said the good-natured sheriff. "I don't want to do you no wrong, man! Hold on, and I'll come and bring him in here. He'll have to be in irons, though!"

"Irons?" said Broom blankly. "Irons? Well, well, let him be in irons, then, if he has to be, but bring him quickly."

Chains rattled as the sheriff, disappearing through the door, took a set off the wall. Then a steel door closed with a jangle, and Mr. Broom, approaching the window still closer, leaned out until he felt the rain soaking through his hair.

He ducked back inside again as the noise of the chains approached the door of the office once more, and in came the sheriff, herding Henry before him. Henry's wrists were locked together by handcuffs, and his ankles were imprisoned by other fetters, while he carried in his hands the heavy leaden ball which was his anchor.

The sheriff regarded them for a moment with a broad grin.

"I hope you get on together all right," said he. "I'm gunna leave you alone for a minute. I reckon that was a rap at the front door of the jail!"

He withdrew, and as he left, Broom hung suspended for an instant between his desire for immediate action, and his fear lest the sheriff should still be within hearing, for the partition was paper-thin. However, the withdrawing steps of the sheriff were now audible, and Broom lunged forward at Henry.

"Henry," he gasped, "if you're set free, you turn back the money to me? You scoundrel! You thief! You turn it back every penny? You'll be an honest man, Henry? Will you give me your promise?"

"Why," drawled Henry slowly, "what the word of a crook and a thief might be worth, I dunno."

"I want your promise. I don't ask anything else. D'you hear me, man?"

"I hear you," said Henry, "though I dunno how you're to get me loose from this unless you've got the keys to the chains!"

"You hear me—will you promise?"

"Why, then," said Henry, "I might promise. I will promise, if that does you any good!"

"You'll swear, man?"

"I'll swear, then, if that makes you rest any easier!"

"Then—" began Broom.

But Henry broke in softly: "Here comes your key, eh?"

Through the window swiftly came Duval's head, his shoulders; then lightly he swung in and dropped to the floor.

"You've got your gun, have you?" he said to Broom.

"I've got it."

Broom pulled out a stub-nosed revolver as he spoke.

"Keep your finger off the trigger," said Duval, dropping to his knees before Henry, and beginning to work deftly on the ankle lock. "Mind when you shoot through the window that you point the muzzle up!"

"I'll mind!" said Broom. "Faster, faster, man! My God, I think he's coming back now—"

"So," said Duval, and the clips sprang loose from the legs of Henry with a soft click.

Duval stood up, and transferred his attention to the prisoner's handcuffs. Scarcely a touch seemed needed; they sprang open; and Duval, locking them shut again, laid them noiselessly on the floor.

"Mind you," he cautioned in a low voice to Broom. "Henry must have slipped the handcuffs, while you were pulling down that first window to shut out the rain—pull it down now, Henry!"

The prisoner obeyed.

He had not spoken since Duval entered, but his appearance had changed. There was light in his dead eyes, and color glowed in his cheeks.

Down dragged the window, screeching as it came.

"And getting the handcuffs off, he must have had some watch spring or other to work on the ankle lock—see! There it is on the floor!"

He threw down a little glittering piece of steel as he spoke.

"Now, Henry, out through the window with you!"

He set the example as he spoke, slithering through the window and dropping to the ground outside. Henry, more slowly, followed him, and as he hung by his hands, there was a tremendous yell from Broom, who sprang to the window and rapidly fired three shots into the air, screeching: "Help! He's away! Help! Help! He's gone! Sheriff Adare! Marshal Kinkaid—"

The door burst open, and the sheriff ran in, white with fear and excitement.

He saw Mr. Broom in a state of frenzy.

"He must have slipped his handcuffs while I was pulling down that damned window against the rain —then a watchspring, maybe, for the ankle lock. Good God, do something man! A hundred and eighty thousand dollars gone forever! Do something! Do something! Are you going to stand there and let him go?"

"What in the name of the Lord did *you* do?" gasped the sheriff. "Stand and watch him go?"

"He slugged me from behind!" said Broom, wringing his hands and dropping his revolver. "I rolled over on the floor and shot after him. I think I hit him. I must have hit him. See if there's any blood on the window sill! I'm sure that I put one bullet right into his breast—"

The sheriff leaned out the window for one look into the blinding mist of the rain, then he turned on his heel with a groan and ran back through the office, tearing down his hat from a peg as he went, and calling over his shoulder:

"You've ruined my name for me! I'll never hear the end of this!"

"Your name, your name!" said Broom to himself, as the sheriff disappeared. "Is it worth a hundred and eighty thousand dollars, more or less honestly made? Is it worth that, you poor snivelling fool!"

And he laughed, in a fierce ecstasy.

In the meantime, nothing was more simple than Duval's and Henry's escape. They retired to the place where the two good horses were waiting, and Henry, as he swung his leg over the cantle of his saddle, made the cooking utensils clang softly together.

"Hey!" he called warily. "Does it mean that I'm away?"

"Away—yes!"

"And you—with me?"

"We're heading for the stuff that you buried. What's the right way?"

"It's not fifty yards from the house. Come along! I thought—for a while—that you were going to be fool enough to turn it back to Broom, if you could!"

"Well, could I?"

"I'd of seen you damned first! A hundred and eighty thousand dollars for that ferret?"

So they went up the side of Moose Creek on the now familiar trail, and as they came nearer to the house, Henry stopped his horse and swung down from it. He worked for only a few moments under the bushes, and emerged again carrying a mud-caked satchel.

"This is the stuff, pal," said he.

"All right," said Duval. "Climb onto your horse. I'll hold it for you."

He took the satchel from the other's hands, and Henry climbed laboriously back into his seat.

"Do we stop at the house for anything else?" asked Henry. "Have we got everything with us? Don't look to me as though you're carrying much of a pack, though!"

"Doesn't it?" answered Duval. "As a matter of fact, I'm not leaving, you see."

"You—ain't—leaving!" cried Henry.

"I'm not leaving. There's something in Moose Creek worth more to me than your hundred and eighty thousand dollars. However, come along and see that I deliver this satchel where it belongs."

"Pal," burst out Henry shakily, "will you tell me the truth? You ain't really meaning to take it away from me?"

"I'm taking it away from you," said Duval.

"I didn't think you was that low!" said Henry. "I can't believe it still. You're only joking with me!"

"Follow me, then, and you'll see!"

Henry, speechless with miserable astonishment, cried: "Not back to Broom! Not back to that rat of a man!"

"Hush, Henry," said Duval. "When you call him names like that, you almost tempt me not to live up to my word. I promised him the money back if you went free."

"Promised him!" shouted Henry. "Besides, Kinkaid would of let me go, for saying who Duval is!"

His anger, his helplessness forced the words from him, and Duval replied gently: "D'you think that Kinkaid really would have let you off, Henry? Don't you know that he couldn't? The most he could have done would have been to arrange a light sentence for you. And any sentence for safecracking would be long enough to see you die in stripes, old fellow. If Kinkaid lied to you, that's no reason that you should lie to yourself!"

To this, poor Henry was unable to make any rejoinder, and he rode on with his head fallen upon his breast.

They kept on up the road for a few miles, then swung aside, and so came down the bypath to Broom's house.

It was lighted down one side. Voices issued dimly from it, and Duval, the satchel across his saddle bow and old Henry not far behind him, rode up beside the nearest window.

It was unshuttered, and the blinds were undrawn, so that he could look freely in, and there he saw Mr. Carson, his fat, rosy face quite pale and long with dismay, while active Mr. Broom, quick-turning as a rat, pranced up and down the room, talking with both hands and with a barking voice.

Apparently he was rehearsing for the benefit of his partner the scene in the sheriff's office, not as it actually had happened, but as Broom had first narrated it to the sheriff himself.

"I suppose it's gone," said Carson, in a voice which Duval, pressing closer, could hear. "You have enough interest in the business to carry you along, but my share of that loss will about squeeze me out!"

"Your own fault!" shouted the unspeakable Broom. "Who told you to cut down expenses? Who told you to cut off that list of ailing paupers that call themselves your relatives? I told you. You wouldn't listen. You been bled white! A fool deserves to stew in his own folly, and you're stewing now. Don't ask me for sympathy! Not a penny's worth of it, for I—"

The window was raised by Duval.

As it squeaked up, and the moist air of the night blew in, Mr. Broom dropped with a groan of fear behind a chair, but Mr. Carson stood up and turned his face and his breast to the possible danger.

However, it was at his feet that Duval cast the satchel, saying briefly: "Here's the stuff back again! It was only Henry's joke!"

Then he was off again into the veil of the night which had covered him even when he was speaking at the lighted window.

Henry fell in beside him in an altered mood, and though he did not speak for some time, he eventually said: 'Look here!"

"Well, Henry?" asked Duval.

"They've got the stuff safe back, then?"

"They have it safely back."

"It was him," said Henry, in a puzzled tone. "I generally keep my promises, but to a rat like him—"

"Why, I understand perfectly," said Duval.

"Well, now that it's been given back to him, I'm pretty glad of it! It's a sort of a funny weight off my mind."

"Is it?"

"I mean, this way. Every penny that I spent of it, I'd have been saying to myself that I was spending another man's money!"

Duval chuckled.

"How much money did you ever spend in your life," he asked, "that was really your own?"

"That ain't what I mean," persisted the thief. "I mean—the money that I spent before, it was stole honestly, if you know what I mean, old-timer?"

"Yes, I know what you mean."

"Not promised back, after I had it. Or anything like that!"

"Certainly," said Duval. "Not on your conscience, you mean? You forgive me then, Henry?"

"Here's my hand, if you can find it in the dark!"

"I never shook hands with more pleasure in my entire life," said Duval cordially. "We'll have no trouble after this, Henry. We understand each other. But now tell me. What are your plans?"

"I dunno. I ain't made any very clear plans, except to skin out from here! I'll go where you go, I suppose."

"Not that, because I stay here, and this is likely to be a pretty hot corner for you, Henry!"

"But you—you ain't really going to stay on here?"

"Yes, I'll stay on here!"

"You mean it?"

"Yes, I mean it."

"But now they'll be after you as thick as hornets!"

"What have they against me?"

"That you kept a professional thief in your house, and so they'll say that you're a professional thief yourself, the fools!"

"Well, perhaps they will. Talking doesn't break the skin, though, as you ought to know."

"I don't like it," muttered Henry, and swinging his horse closer to the mare, he went on: "You'd better slide out with me! I know how to make tracks from here so's they'll never guess."

"They'll know that I've run, though, and that's the same as a confession of guilt. Isn't it?"

"Damn the guilt! What's the guilt that they could trace back to you?"

"I mean, I'll appear guilty, and beaten, and afraid!"

"Mr.—"

"Not even in the dark, Henry. Not that name even to ourselves!"

"All right, then. I won't say it. But it looks to me as though you're running a fine chance of bein' tagged by a forty-five caliber slug one of these days. I've had my chance to look around the world and see my share of the hard ones, but I never saw a harder one than Kinkaid."

"Would he murder me, Henry?"

"Would a cat eat cream?"

"He would, I think," said Duval thoughtfully. "I think he'd kill me out of hand. As a matter of fact, for the first time in my life I'm afraid of a man—afraid of the marshal! But still I have to stay, even though I know the danger."

"Will you tell me why you *have* to stay?"

"I can't tell you. I can't begin to tell you, Henry. You've lived past certain things which still are real to me. Things that are as much a part of me, now, as my own blood."

Henry was silent for a moment, and then he muttered: "There's such a thing as playing a game till it ain't a game any longer. It's real. And you're that man, I suppose!"

21

Duval stopped in front of Pete's Place at high noon and dismounted. He looked up and down the street, but not a form was stirring. Only, in the distance, he heard the mellow clangor of the blacksmith's hammer, sounding musically far away and soothing.

There were two or three other noticeable things, chiefly faint shadows which stirred behind windows, discreetly disappearing; these, he knew, were the heads of the curious who had looked out upon him, but who did not wish to be seen.

It meant much to him, for it told him that he had become outlawed from the notice of frank, everyday life. He was a banned and forbidden thing, and he could guess that it was because of Henry's arrest and then his flight. That had damned him; with the whispers concerning beautiful Marian Lane as a background against which the most recent and spectacular action was placed in relief.

Duval turned back into the saloon, and passing through the door, he saw Charlie Nash, not at the bar but seated at a small table with his head in his hands.

He started toward Charlie with a smile, but Pete,

behind the bar, raised a warning hand and shook his head.

That instant Charlie looked up, and seeing Duval, rose from his chair, shoved his hat back on his head, and came straight up to the older man. Not a word of greeting did he speak and Duval wondered.

When he spoke it was to say in a harsh, husky voice: "Who are you?"

"My name," said he, "is Duval. I am a citizen of the United States. I generally vote Republican. My height is five feet eleven. My weight is a hundred and sixty-five pounds. My hair is brown, and my eyes are gray. Nose, acquiline. Mouth, medium. Chin, medium. Characteristic marks, hardly any worth mentioning. Does that answer you, Charlie?"

Charlie Nash groaned.

"I might of known that it would be something like that," he said.

But he did not give back. The aggressiveness remained in his attitude.

"What else can I tell you, Charlie?"

"A lot, if you'll talk!"

"Oh, I'll talk!"

"Then tell me the straight of it—God knows that I haven't been askin' questions about it before— but whatcha mean about Marian Lane?"

"She'll tell you a lot better than I can, Charlie."

"How can I ask her? You know that! I'm askin' you!"

"I know you're asking me. What's your right to ask, Charlie?"

"The right of lovin' her. The right of havin' stood to be your friend. If them two reasons ain't enough," he continued, raising his voice.

"If you want to know about Marian Lane, will you come over to the store with me? I'm gunna talk to her now."

"Are you tryin' to make a fool out of me?"

"Me? Not a bit! I'm goin' over there to find out what I can do with her!"

"Duval, you ain't stringin' her? You mean to marry her?"

"What I mean don't count much with her. It's what she means that seems to be a lot more important."

Charlie laughed sardonically.

"As if you couldn't twist her or anybody around your finger! Only—what lies in front of you, Duval? What're you gunna offer to her? Is it straight that Henry was a crook? Are you a crook, too? Where'd you get your money? Where'd you come from? What's behind you? Where are you goin'? Is it a fact that Kinkaid is after you?"

"Why, you want me to talk and talk," said Duval, smiling. "Fact is, everything hangs on what Marian says to me!"

Charlie Nash gritted his teeth. "Is it because you sure care about her, Duval? Ain't it because she's the only one in Moose Creek that's stood out much agin you? Ain't it because you wanta show how strong you are with women, the same as you've showed how strong you are with men? Either you come clean to me, or else I'm gunna block your game with Marian. That's the fact."

"As far as runnin' away with her goes," said Duval, "I ain't likely to do that, old son, till tonight. Suppose that you come up and have supper with me in my shack. Will you do that?"

"If you'll talk!"

"I'll talk, well enough."

"I'll come," said Charlie.

"Then have a drink with me."

Duval went behind the bar.

"What'll it be, partner? Red-eye or beer? Or red-eye with a beer chaser? What'll you have?"

"I'll eat with you tonight," said Charlie. "I won't drink with you now. I'm sick and sore inside of my heart, Duval. I dunno where I stand. I ain't no use to myself. I ain't no use to the girl I want for a wife. But by God, I'm gunna try to do one thing, if I die for it!"

He turned his back and walked from the saloon, while Duval looked earnestly after him.

After a small whisky, he tossed off a chaser of water and started for the door. A voice called cautiously behind him, as though fearing lest an unexpected ear might overhear it. It was Pete, coming toward him with an extended hand, which Duval freely gripped.

"Duval," said Pete, "I dunno what's gunna come of all of this. Somehow, I work it out that there ain't gunna be a long stay for you with us, after all of this trouble. When I first seen you come into this here bar, I aimed to say that you wasn't the kind that waited long around one joint. But when you leave us, Duval, whenever that may be, I wanta say that my wishes go along with you. Good luck to you, man, a hoss that'll never quit, and a gun that'll never miss!"

With that farewell in his ears, he crossed the street rapidly and entered Marian Lane's store.

It was a rush hour in the Lane Store, for there were three or four patrons, including a girl with a whipping pigtail, waiting to buy red-striped peppermint candies. The others completed their purchases in haste and left the store at once with their eyes discreetly lowered to the floor, but the little girl, as she went out with her mouth stuffed with the sweets, backed through the door, still gaping openly at the most famous man of Moose Creek.

The door shut with a slam behind her, and Duval could pay his attention to Marian Lane.

Her usual manner of baby-faced sweetness she abandoned the instant they were alone, standing back against the wall with her hands folded behind her and looking rather wearily at Duval.

"This," said he, "is the biggest compliment I've ever received."

"Is it, David?" said she. "What sort of a compliment?"

"You've swept up all your little mannerisms and put them away, and here is the real Marian Lane watching me, a little tired, as I guess by the shadows under her eyes, but finally fairly honest!"

"D'you want honesty, David?"

"Of course I do, as long as it's pleasant."

"And suppose it isn't?"

"I don't want to suppose that. Everything leads me to think that you're more amiable today, my dear."

"How do you come to that conclusion, then?"

"Because you're almost beaten. In the game we've been playing."

"I'm not a whit beaten!"

"See, now," he said cruelly. "You're trembling a little."

"I haven't slept much, and my nerves are a little upset. That's all."

"But still you're beaten. You haven't done the thing that you wanted to do."

"Will you tell me what that is, then?"

"Of course I shall. You set out to find out all about me. You've managed to drive me out of the town, but you haven't learned."

She started, almost imperceptibly.

"Are you going to leave us, David?"

"I am."

"Forever?"

"It matters a little, I see," he remarked, without exultation.

"Yes, it matters a good deal. Moose Creek is going to seem pretty cramped and small without you."

"Thank you," said Duval.

"You knocked out the walls and made us live in a bigger house," she admitted, "but of course before the summer's over, it will have burned away everything except a dim memory of you."

"Not dim in you, Marian."

"No?"

"Not a whit dim in you. You'll remember me to your death day!"

"That's not like you," said the girl, in her curiously cold, judicial manner which she often showed when she was with Duval. "You don't often show any vanity."

"It isn't vanity. It's the most profound humility. But I think that it's fair to say that a girl never forgets any man who has thrown himself at her feet."

At this, she scanned him a little more closely still, and finally smiled.

"Have you thrown yourself at my feet?" she asked.

"Deliberately, passionately, wildly," said Duval, yawning a little.

"Have you made yourself a fool about me?"

"Tell me, Marian. Have I let you scorn me, treat me with contempt, baffle me, hunt me down with your hired men?"

"Hired men?" she echoed. "Hired men?"

"Certainly! Hired by the hope that you would at least smile at them, hired by the trust that you would reward them by taking them in as friends! Am I wrong?"

She did not answer.

"This is my day for frankness," said Duval. "Will you make it your day, also?"

"Well," she said, "I must play with you that far. Yes, they were hired, then, if you wish to put it that way!"

"Thank you," said Duval. "We'll get on, at this rate! Then you admit that you've pursued me with horses and hounds, as it were, and whips and guns?"

She shrugged her shoulders

"For no other reason than because I wouldn't tell you who I was?"

"You know that that's only a part of the reason."

"Well, perhaps. However, you know that you've had me dodging."

"Yes. A little. But never very far. Never enough to make me think that you were being driven away."

"Driven from my house and my farm, that I've invested so much labor in?"

"That's a harsh way to put it. I never intended that, and I haven't done that!"

"Haven't you?"

"No."

"If I prove it, will you admit that I'm right?"

"Well, perhaps."

"Look here, Marian. What has driven me away?"

"I suppose you mean on account of Henry's arrest, his escape—I wonder how you managed that! —and because the idiots think that you're what Henry is! But why should untrue things like that drive you away?"

"Because they now think that I'm a thief, like Henry, why should that drive me away?"

"Exactly!"

"I'll tell you a few good reasons. One of them is that every man jack in the county who has anything against me would not hesitate to take a crack at me with my back turned, now. I'm under the shadow. I'm no longer wanted. That's the reason. This is dangerous hunting ground if I'm the fox and all the others are hounds."

"You can't blame all of that on me!"

"Distinctly and definitely I can. Without you, Kinkaid never would have taken up my trail."

"Are you back at that?"

"Of course I am. You expected it, you dreaded it, that's why you pretend that the subject wearies you. Am I right?"

She pursed her lips in contemplation, and frowned a little. Then, impatiently, she rubbed the wrinkles out of her forehead and exclaimed: "You'd make an old woman of me in another month, with your talk, David!"

"You haven't answered me."

"I don't intend to answer."

"That's all right. I'll accept every point that's

surrendered in this manner. But now to continue, in spite of all of this hounding that I've received, here I am throwing myself at your feet, Marian."

"Oh, stuff and nonsense," said the girl.

"Literally at your feet, disregarding the insults and the dangers which you've thrown in my way."

"At my feet!" said she, "and there I see you, almost yawning in my face, criticizing me, analyzing me like a chemical compound, telling yourself that I'm looking a trifle old today, that I'll wither young, that after all, it's not a very interesting flirtation that you're about to leave behind you, making a last summing up of poor Marian Lane, and her poor little store, in the wretched little town of Moose Creek!"

"The fact is," said Duval, "that we're horribly alike in most ways, and that's why we'll miss one another."

"That's not according to the proverb, which says that unlikes attract one another."

"Only in a stupid way, however. Opposites are attracted by the essential mystery. They remain in love, for instance, until they know each other better. But people who are alike have ended the most miserable necessity in life before it becomes a levelled gun at their heads."

"What miserable necessity?"

"That of confession, which overwhelms us, otherwise, from time to time, and makes us talk our hearts out and then feel degraded, but lighter about the conscience."

"You and I, for instance?"

"We know one another—the cynicism, the scoffing, the cruelty, the lightness, the bitter selfishness. We understand, we know that we are understood, and therefore we are at ease. Pain is removed. Will you grant that?"

She hesitated. Then he insisted: "That's why it's a restful and a delightful thing to be with one another?"

At this, she nodded. "And that's why," she answered, "it's absurd for you to speak of being at my feet."

"Is it? Let me show you."

With that, he vaulted over the counter and dropped to his knees before her.

He took her hands as she would have recoiled from him.

"Here you see me, Marian, literally on my knees, my heart bowed down, in the dust of your persecution, your contempt, telling you that I couldn't do without you, that I would miss you more—"

"Than coffee in the morning?"

"Are you going to keep on scoffing, and force me to be poetic, eloquent, and pitiful? Or will you leave me a few shreds of self-respect?"

"I'll leave you your self-respect, if you'll go back across the counter."

Instantly he was on the farther side of it, his eyes glittering at her with triumph and excitement.

"At least I've made you take me almost seriously!" said he.

"Yes, you have—almost! What is it you want to do with me, David?"

"Take you away with me!"

"Where?"

"Wherever luck and adventure lead us!"

"Shall I tell you where that would be?"

"Tell me what you guess."

"Your home is back East, perhaps out on Long Island, surrounded with big lawns, gardens, gardeners, stables, grooms; inside there is a gray-haired lady, your mother, a frosty aunt, with a professional smile, and everything prepared to overwhelm and crush poor Marian Lane."

He drummed his fingers on the counter top.

"Suppose that that were not true, Marian?"

"Well?"

"Would you take me seriously? Would you go off with me and give yourself a chance to fall in love?"

An odd warmth came into her musing eyes, and in her daydream she looked aside, out of the window. That instant, her glance changed, and she was shocked back to reality.

"No!" said the girl.

Duval, following the direction of her look, saw through the window the looming bulk of Marshal Dick Kinkaid, who now turned into the store.

"Is it the marshal, then?" said Duval, contempt in his voice. "Does that hard-handed brute of a man mean so much to you?"

"You'd better go," said the girl. "I think that he wants to say something to me!"

"On the contrary, I'll stay," said Duval, "because I have something to say to him!"

Kinkaid went to the counter in the most casual manner, nodded to the girl, overlooked Duval, and asked for bacon and cornmeal, a few pounds of each.

Dust lay thick on his shoulders and in the creases of his trousers; since rain had fallen the night before, it was plain that he had been riding far away.

One had a sense of fatigue about him, too, although there was so much iron in the man that it did not readily strike the eye; it was rather felt than seen.

"Well, Dick," said Duval, "I see that you've forgotten me?"

Kinkaid did not even turn his head.

"If you'll wrap that up in some of the oiled paper," he was saying to the girl. He added: "I remember you, somewhere. I sort of forget your real name, though!"

Then Duval said slowly: "I'm giving a little supper party at my shack tonight. Charlie Nash is coming. I hope that you two will both come. D'you accept, Kinkaid?"

He did not answer.

"Marian is going to be there," said Duval smoothly. "And I thought that you might enjoy being present at my last appearance in Moose Creek, Kinkaid?"

Still the marshal did not speak.

"Silence I'll take for polite acceptance. Because, after you've turned the matter over in your agile brain for a time, you'll understand why you must be there, Richard. So good-bye until that happy time. By the way, you might ask your chum along, if you care to—I mean, Larry Jude!"

With that Parthian shot, he retreated from the store, swung onto Cherry, and disappeared at once down the street.

The marshal continued to stare out of the window, until the dust which the mare had raised in her gallop blew past or settled down again. Then he turned to Marian Lane.

He pointed. "You're going up the hill, tonight?"

She shrugged her shoulders, studying him.

His voice rose as he spoke, against his will booming loud and ominous.

And she, watching him with her head canted a little to one side, and an almost meaningless smile on her lips, said: "I hadn't heard his invitation until you came in, Dick."

"He hadn't asked you, then? You hadn't said you'd go?" asked the marshal, eagerly.

She nodded.

"But of course I'd better go with you, Dick!"

The pleasant poison ran warmly through his veins.

Still, through a hot haze, he talked sense to her: "Y'understand that it's a challenge that he's sending to me, Marian?"

"I suppose it is, in a way!"

"A sneakin', low challenge, askin' you along to see that there's no real trouble starts? I never figgered it before, but I can see now that he's afraid of me, and by the Lord, he's gunna have reason for his fear!"

"Not tonight, Dick!"

"Tonight? In front of a woman? No, not tonight! There's plenty of days afterward."

She nodded, still thoughtful, only murmuring: "I wouldn't be sure that he's afraid of anyone—hardly even of you, Dick!"

"Marian, they's one grand job on my hands—Duval! I gotta finish that job, and when it's done—mind you, you steered me onto it!—then I'm gunna have something to say to you that'll mean something. D'you understand?"

"You're goin' up there with him, Marian, to his house?"

She did not answer.

"What I'd like to know now, is there any sort of a hope for me, that you'd take me serious, I mean? I ain't a man that can talk, say pretty things, play the fool around a woman. But you've opened the door and stepped inside of my brain, Marian. You're lodged there, and I could never get you out. D'you believe it?"

She answered suddenly: "I couldn't doubt a thing you say that way."

"You couldn't answer me now?" asked the marshal, leaning his elbows on the counter, so that suddenly his bulk was impending over her.

In spite of herself, she glanced up with a frightened widening of her eyes.

Kinkaid was instantly himself again, and standing erect at a little distance.

"I dunno how to talk, I dunno how to do," said he. "I got no kind of manners, honey, but I could sort of learn."

"Yes," she said faintly.

So he loved her, but Duval?

There was a different matter. If he cared at all, it was because he saw her almost more clearly than she saw herself. When she was with him, she felt his sensitive intelligence surround and embrace her mind and her spirit. She was, in a sense, in his hand. And, if she could have felt the same possession of him, would she have hesitated one instant before telling him that she, also, loved him, and far more truly than ever he could care for her?

Out of this musing she was drawn by the marshal's voice.

"I been blunt—too fast—too straight to the point—and I gotta give you time—a kid like you, as though you could make up your mind about a gent like me so quick!"

He retreated a little as he spoke, then came suddenly forward to her.

"There's one thing else that I better say to you now."

He took from his coat pocket a chamois bag, drawn tight at the mouth with leather strings.

"We started to know each other on account of Duval," said the marshal. "And it's only right that I should tell you now that I figger that I have a lot concernin' him here in this. What's more, he knows that I have it, and there ain't gunna be a minute of my life, until he's dead or gone, that'll find me safe and easy so long as he knows that I still got this."

He paused, then he went on: "You dunno what's in it. I'd like to have you tell me that you won't look, either!"

She nodded, intensely, feverishly curious and excited.

"The reason that I give it to you is just what I say —that I dunno whether I'll get to the end of the day or not! If I don't—and if you get the word to you that I been snagged somewhere, and killed, nobody knows by who—you'll take this here bag to the sheriff. He's kind of two-thirds a fool, but he's mighty honest, and he's got a good deal of experience. He'll know how to use what's in there, and maybe it'll be from old Nat Adare that you'll hear the truth about this here Duval!"

He ended uneasily, and mopped his wet face with a colored handkerchief.

"I reckon that that's about all, Marian."

"I'll keep it as safe—as my eyes!" said the girl earnestly.

"Ay. I guess you will. I'd trust you, Marian! Tonight I'll come for you right after sundown, and we'll go up the hill together, the way that you said!"

22

Duval was intently at work with a reddened face above his stove. For he had on half a dozen little tins in which he was stewing various ingredients to make a sauce.

It was after he had straightened from this occupation that he heard a throat cleared outside his door.

"Hello?" said Duval, without turning.

"You forgot the salad," said Henry's voice as he entered the cabin, his hands filled with greens.

Duval stiffened, but did not look around from his cookery.

"Well, Henry," said he, "did the horse break a leg?"

"No, he didn't break a leg. He's a return-horse, though."

"How did you find that out?"

"I was drifting along through the hills," said Henry, "and let the reins hang loose, so's I could think a little better. And pretty soon I come to out of my thoughts—"

"What were your thoughts, Henry?"

"That I was getting old; that I was getting mighty old!"

"Not too old to use a can opener on old-fashioned safes, Henry."

"But too old to cover my tracks!"

"Yes, you made a fairly clumsy job of it!"

"Too old to keep out of jail! So old," went on Henry, "that I had to take charity money to live on."

"Not charity money, Henry. Friendship money, which I was glad to lend you, or give you, whichever way you'll take it!"

"Charity money," insisted Henry, "from the same man that I came out here to blackmail, that took me in, treated me white, and then got me out of jail after I'd spoiled his game and made a fool of myself!"

Duval whistled.

"You have the blues badly. You were saying that you'd waked out of these thoughts of yours—?"

"And found out that the horse had turned and was wandering back in the direction we'd come from, so I simply let him come, and he wound up here!"

"Hello! That's interesting."

"Seemed to me that it meant I should stay where I was," said Henry. "That's as much as to say, with you!"

"And so here you are?"

"Yes."

"When did you come?"

"A good while before dark."

"Take a hand here and baste the roast, will you?" said Duval.

He gathered up the dishes in which he had been cooking the sauce, and put them far back on the stove, where they would only simmer, very slowly.

In the meantime, Henry was basting the roast, and singing softly in spite of the steam that rolled out into his face.

"There's still old Kinkaid," observed Duval.

"Yeah?" drawled the old man, as though without interest in this remark.

"He's quite alive," said Duval, "and he's coming here tonight."

"Be glad to see him again," said Henry. "In sort of a social way, as you might say!"

Duval began to laugh, working at the salad.

"Henry," said he, "whenever I feel myself growing old, you say something that makes me young again. Henry, without you, life would soon become intolerably dull. You're intending to stay here and face the marshal, are you?"

"They got that law of hospitality out here in the West," remarked Henry, "and I suppose that he wouldn't be breaking that and getting himself a bad name all over the range?"

"Is that what you trust to?"

"There's another law that I trust to," admitted Henry.

"What's that?"

"The law of Duval!"

At this point, the younger man turned toward him with a broad smile.

"You're a diplomat, old fellow," said he. "You can turn me around your finger without the slightest effort. There's no one in the world like you, Henry. Very well. Stay on, then. As a matter of fact, I begin to see that you can be of help to me. There's someone coming up the lane; see who it is!"

Henry went to the door and instantly said over

his shoulder: "Not Kinkaid!"

"It's Charlie Nash, then."

"Nash, too?"

"Ay, and Marian Lane."

Henry whistled.

"No wonder you want me, then," said he, "to keep yourself from being talked down. Nash is walkin' pretty slow. You'd think that he was carrying a load!"

"He is," said Duval. "His brain is loaded so deep that you couldn't see the Plimsoll line. Be kind to Charlie, because he's young, and means better than he can do!"

"Ay," said Henry. "He's one of them that nearly win every race but trip on their own heels at the finish. He'd be a champion if he wasn't a dub. Here he is!"

An instant later Charlie Nash's voice sounded at the door.

"Come in!" said Henry. "Come right in and make yourself at home, will you?"

"Sure," said Charlie, a little uncertain.

He stepped in through the door and exclaimed: "Henry! You still here?"

"The chief wanted me to help him serve up this dinner," said Henry in careful explanation. "So I stayed a while, not thinkin' that the marshal would miss a meal like this to keep ridin' after me!"

Charlie Nash looked around, bewildered. He saw the table laid for four, and his bewilderment increased greatly at the sight of it.

"Duval," he said, "is Kinkaid coming here, by what Henry says?"

"We hope he won't be rushed too much by business to let him come," said Duval hopefully.

Nash threw himself into a chair and drew a great breath.

"Tired?" asked Duval.

"No, happy!"

"Glad to hear it."

"I been sayin' good-bye to the world all the way up the hill!"

"Good-bye?"

"Why, Duval, don't blink at me as if you didn't understand! You know what I came up here for tonight!"

"Supper, of course!"

"Ay," growled Charlie, "as much supper as the marshal is comin' for, but if he's gunna be in the center of the stage, I won't have to be bothered."

"Right!" said Duval pleasantly. "You're to be the spectator this evening, Charlie."

"And the fourth place is for Henry?"

"No, sir," said Henry. "I'm the butler tonight, because the gents are going to eat in style, with a lady."

"Lady?"

"Yes."

"Ah," said Nash, with a great gasp. "Duval, don't tell me that I'm right when I say that it's gunna be Marian Lane?"

"Yes, she's promised to let Kinkaid bring her up the hill!"

"Great God!" breathed Charlie Nash, and sat silently for a moment, his face bright with perspiration.

"I might have guessed that everything would be over my head," he said at last.

"Not over your head," said Duval, reassuringly. "I want you here as a neutral, to look on. Besides, you may reap a fine harvest out of this here!"

"Harvest?"

"Why, if the marshal and me kill each other, it leaves you pretty clear in possession of the field, don't it?"

23

Henry had disappeared to fetch a fresh bucket of water; both Nash and Duval were busy at odd jobs about the cookery when Marian Lane stepped across the threshold of the cabin with the great shadow of the marshal behind her.

The house was very gay. Some late blossoming shrubs had been ravished to secure decorations, and the wind which passed through the door stirred the scent of the flowers gently through the room.

Marian Lane would have begun helping at once, and even the marshal gloomily offered to contribute his assitance, but Duval refused all help.

So they were ushered to their chairs. She had the one available upright chair for the table. The marshal was favored with a stool which had no back, and Duval and Charlie Nash had empty boxes which needed some attention to keep them from slumping to one side or the other.

Soup began the meal, a soup with a most luscious flavor, and they fell on it. Their manners were all worth attention, the girl in the first place being all smiles, turning from one to another with the most cheerful remarks. These were answered by

Charlie Nash in an embarrassed manner. Charlie was on his dignity, as one unwilling to give away a trick, no matter in what formidable company he found himself, and he was so earnestly devoted to keeping his chin in and his back straight and his brows slightly bent, that he could hardly speak.

The marshal made little pretense of hearing anything, for he was all eyes. In the first place, before sitting down he had looked all around him and made sure that the wall was at his back; next he attacked the soup with care, as though he suspected that poison might be in it. And he was continually looking up from it sharply, as though he expected to surprise Duval in the midst of a telltale gesture or glance. At the same time, he was terribly ill at ease, for he felt that he was not appearing to the best advantage in the presence of the girl. Certainly he was at his worst compared with the smiling ease of Duval, who had a word for everyone, and singlehanded sustained the conversation with the girl.

The soup was ended for the marshal, who now rested his big elbows on the edge of the table and was sullenly on his guard, when the tall, meager form of Henry appeared in the doorway.

A totally irresistible instinct at once ruled the marshal. He could not help snapping out his revolver and covering the man he wanted so badly.

"Hello, Marshal Kinkaid," said Henry, smiling broadly. "I'm glad to see you here, sir. Are you seein' a bear behind me?"

He glanced over his shoulder, as though he imagined that the other must have taken aim at an enemy behind him.

Charlie Nash had sprung up and almost upset

the table at the first flash of the Colt, but Duval raised a deprecatory hand.

"Kinkaid, Kinkaid," said he in gentle reproval. "It ain't hardly right, is it, to scare the lady before she's finished her soup?"

The marshal was slowly rising.

"I want him. He belongs to me!" said Kinkaid with much conviction. "I've had him once, and now I'll have him again, and he'll have the stripes on before I ever let him out of my sight agin!"

"Suppose, Kinkaid," said Duval, "that Henry had wanted to work out his grudge against you. He had a pretty good target through the door, eh?"

The marshal grunted, as this thrust told.

Then, baffled, his glance wavered as far as the girl's face.

"This night, Dick," she said persuasively, "there's not to be any trouble, is there? And Henry's such an old man!"

"You've brought him here and shoved him under my nose!" said Kinkaid explosively to Duval. "What's the meaning of that, I'd like to know?"

"My old man," Duval said, "always used to say that a gent that had to wait on himself never had no appetite for what he had before him, and I figgered out that Henry would be right useful here to hand the things round. And Henry don't mind!"

"Not a bit," said Henry, whose smile would not go off. "Matter of fact, I'd do almost anything to keep the marshal feelin' cheerful."

He was picking up the dishes as he spoke, and the marshal slowly lowered the weapon to its holster.

He was infinitely sorry for two reasons.

The first and less important was that he had exhibited vicious and unmannerly temper in the presence of the girl; and having begun a job he had not finished it. The second reason was that he had given to Duval a chance to time with his eye exactly the speed of the marshal's draw.

And Duval certainly did not appear dismayed by what he saw! On the contrary, the marshal could have sworn that his sly enemy was secretly smiling in content!

Old Henry had cleared away the soup and brought on the next course. But the marshal hardly knew what was before him. Back in his mind rumbled his oath of office like distant thunder, and his head swam with this impossibility—that his fugitive from justice should be here before him, and yet untouched. And always there persisted the sense that he had been trapped.

There was more clearing of the table, rattling of washed dishes, and then the presentation of a great saddle of venison. The marshal heard Marian Lane exclaiming over it, and he stared at her heavily, for it seemed a miracle that she could abandon herself so heartily to enjoyment of that dinner without feeling the danger that was in the air.

Yet, when he looked at her with clearer eyes, he saw that she, too, had forced her pleasure.

They came to coffee, at last, and as they reached this, the marshal's head cleared entirely: he knew what he would do, and drained off the steaming hot contents of the cup at a draught. Then he struck the table with his hand, so that the dishes upon it jumped.

Charlie Nash started violently and uttered a low cry; the girl merely stiffened in her chair.

"Friends," said the marshal, "it's been a fine

party, and I ain't denyin' that. Never sat down to a better meal, but they's a time come when I gotta go back to my job, and the first sign of it is that I gotta take Henry with me. Henry, put on your hat, because you're comin' back to the jail with me! We'll make you right comfortable there!"

"Sure," said Henry. "I'll go along, if the boss can spare me from the job here."

"The boss," said the marshal, looking not at Henry but at Duval, "ain't the man for you to talk to now. It's me that counts here, Henry!"

And suddenly he rejoiced, for he knew that he had brought on the climax that had been impending.

Duval was shaking his head.

"I'd like to let you have him, Kinkaid," said Duval, "but if you put yourself in my boots, you'll see how it is—I can't turn him over to the jail when there are still—so many dirty dishes to be washed, man!"

He smiled amiably at Kinkaid, and the latter flushed heavily. "I dunno what you're drivin' at, Duval," said he, "if it ain't trouble! And if that's what you want—"

"Tut!" said Duval. "It ain't trouble that I want but trouble that I gotta have."

Marian Lane stood up from her chair hastily.

"You don't mean that you'll force things, Dick?" she gasped.

"I been brought here like a fool. I been set down here with that crook, Henry, under my eye. Something's been planned agin' me, and I dunno what. But I do know that Henry's goin' back to the jail with me this night or else—"

"Sit down, Marian," invited Duval. "There ain't

gunna be no trouble until you've finished your coffee, and maybe that'll take you another ten minutes. Let's see. It's twelve minutes to eight, now. Say we make it eight, marshal?"

"Eight for what?" asked big Kinkaid.

"Wind up the clock, will you?" said Duval to Henry, "and set the alarm for eight o'clock. That ought to do for a signal, Kinkaid, eh?"

"A signal for what?" asked Charlie Nash.

"For the shooting," answered Duval.

"Is this another of your bluffs and your fakes?" asked the marshal fiercely. "The thing that wore down Larry Jude will never wear me down!"

"That's a tolerable ornery and hostile way of putting it," answered Duval. "Why, I ain't upsetting you. All I'm doing is saying that we gotta give Marian time to finish her coffee."

Charlie Nash broke in: "Marian, I'm going to take you out of this. Duval means what he says!"

"No, no—" began Marian Lane.

"She'll stay here," said Duval, drawling the words. "Now that she's started the fun, she'd better stay and see the game finish out."

This suggestion struck everyone with amazement.

There was a silence, broken by the creaking of the alarm clock as Henry wound up the spring and adjusted the hand.

It was he who first spoke.

"It'll go off in about ten minutes," said Henry.

"Ten minutes makes a long time, when one wishes to settle up his last affairs," remarked Duval. "You agree to that, Kinkaid?"

"I agree to anything," said the marshal. "Except you're a fool and a brute, if you wanta keep the girl here. Keep her here? This is between you and me. Marian, you go—Nash, take her away!"

"Charlie won't take her away," declared Duval, steadily looking into the white face of the girl. "He'll leave her here where she belongs. I reckon that she even wants to stay. Don't you, Marian?"

He smiled at her.

"Do you mean that you're going to stay here in this room and murder one another?" cried the girl. "Charlie—Henry—"

"No murder—no murder!" said Duval. "Because I aim to state the two of us are both first-rate experts. Him that's the fastest is the one that'll win. The first bullet home will be the only bullet shot. It'll be neat, quick, and pretty. Only one of us will drop, and that's likely to be me, the marshal bein' as you might say a professional—well, man-hunter, you might call him. Bounty-getter! You must of piled up quite considerable, Dick, takin' scalps?"

"I've heard enough of your damn lingo," said Kinkaid. "Get Marian out of the house. Nash can take her. Then you an' me'll finish it out, and the less talkin' the better!"

"Not with Marian gone," said Duval. "You sure want to stay, don't you?"

"Stay? I?" cried the girl. "David—Richard—"

She ended her appeal before it began. "Oh, Charlie," she said, "is there nothing that can be done?"

"Listen at her," said Duval admiringly, "Now you'd think, to listen to her, that she hadn't worked all of this up in good style! You'd think that it wasn't her that put Dick Kinkaid on my trail. You'd think that it wasn't her that started all this trouble, and now that the showdown is about to come, she blanches a mite, and throws up her hands, and hollers how terrible it is, but down in your heart, Marian, you sure must hanker a lot to see this fight!"

"Leave her alone!" thundered the marshal. "You're drivin' her sick with your fool talk. You—"

She had, in fact, slipped limply down into her chair, white and shaking.

"You talk like a grandmama," said Duval to the marshal. "She wanted to see could Duval be licked, and now she's gunna find out and watch with her own eyes!"

He turned to the girl.

"Tell us true, Marian. Ain't that the fact?"

"No!" she cried at him. "I only wanted to know —but whatever my reason was, I see that it was wrong. It *is* my fault! David, if I go on my knees to you and beg you—"

Duval laughed and turning to Henry asked: "What's the time now, Henry?"

"Six minutes left, sir," said Henry.

"Thank you," said Duval. "Now, Kinkaid, we got six minutes left, and maybe you got some affairs that you'd like to put in order?"

Kinkaid sneered broadly.

"I see the game that you're workin'," he declared. "First you're gunna have the girl here, and Charlie. And second, you're gunna make a long wait to break my nerve. It'd work with most, but it won't work with me! I see through you, Duval!"

"Do you?" said Duval patiently. "But if you got friends, family, relations, you'd better think of 'em now. You could tell Charlie. Charlie would remember. Short messages would be the best, though."

"Fill your hand!" answered the marshal, "and we'll finish this off now!"

"There's still coffee in her cup," said Duval. "Besides, I ain't in any hurry. Charlie, have you got a gun?"

"Yes," said Charlie, barely able to speak.

"Pull the gun and stand over agin the wall."

"What for?"

"For seein' that this here fight comes off fair and square. They's a time when that alarm begins that it makes a purrin', like a cat lappin' milk. Then comes the ring. If one of us was to draw a gun before ringin' began, shoot him through the head, Charlie!"

Charlie did not hesitate. He walked like an automaton to the side of the room, and drew his long Colt, grimly ready for action.

"What's the time, Henry?" asked Duval.

"Four minutes, sir."

"Four minutes left," said Duval. "You ain't gunna accept my invitation after all, Dick?"

"Your invitation be damned."

"All right," said Duval, "but it looks to me like you're pretty tense, old-timer. The old man used to say that even steel could get tempered too hard, and then you could break it in your hands! I wouldn't like to see you break like that—not right here in front of Marian and Charlie. The other time, that was different. There was only me and Henry to watch that!"

He smiled genially, and the marshal flared up with hot passion.

"You lie!" said he. "There wasn't no other time!"

"Hush!" said Duval. "There's a lady with us, Dick."

He turned to the girl.

"Now that I am a coupla steps from dyin', maybe, I wanta say in front of the world that I loved you, Marian, mighty nigh from the first time that I laid eyes on you. But you threw a scare into me, at first. You knew a pile too much—"

"Leave her be!" said Kinkaid. "Your time's drawed pretty fine. Leave her be, and if you got talkin' to do, talk to me, Duval, you sneak, you thief, you faker!"

"What time is it, Henry?" said Duval.

"They's about a minute and a half left," said Henry.

"One moment," said Duval. "I sure don't wanta die like this, like a farmer just in from the plough. I mean to say. Gimme a necktie, Henry!"

Duval rapidly donned the necktie, given him by Henry and then jerked down and smoothed his coat. He passed his hand over his hair and turned his pale, smiling face to the girl.

"Do I look better now, Marian?"

She could not speak.

Frozen with white horror, she watched him. He saw her swallow and make a mighty effort, but the words would not come.

"What time is it, Henry?" came Duval's remorselessly polite voice.

"One minute, sir!"

"Now, Kinkaid, there's one minute left for any message you might wanta send."

Kinkaid caught his breath audibly. "Charlie!"

"Ay?" said Charlie Nash.

"My uncle, Tom Chalmers in Butte. Send him word that when I died, I said that I never set 'em on the right trail after his boy Les. But if I live, damn him if I'll give him that comfort. He can think what he wants about me and—"

He clipped off the words sharply, for he knew that the time was coming quickly, and he did not wish to be caught unaware.

"Even Dick Kinkaid had one message to leave behind him," smiled Duval. "What time is it now, Henry!"

"There's less than half a minute," said Henry, "and God help you, Mr.—"

Even then the word was not spoken, not that Duval interfered, but because the alarm machinery began to purr softly, with light clicking.

Then Duval heard the girl cry out in a voice like that of a child, in protest. He himself leaned back a little, and made himself smile straight at the marshal, down whose face he saw the great sweatdrops trickling.

"Why blast the house to pieces?" said Duval. "One shot apiece had oughta be enough, Dick. Here's my five!"

He broke his gun and deliberately rolled five shells out on the table.

"Damn you!" said Kinkaid. His fingers stumbled and shook with nasty fear, but he accepted that last challenge, at that last instant, and breaking his gun, shook out five of the shells.

Instantly he thrust the weapon back into its holster, duly to keep the rules of the game, and as he did so, he saw Duval fold his arms.

It was a final, consummate act of bravado on

Duval's part, or was it real contempt for his enemy, and confidence in himself?

That instant the alarm bell clanged! And with an explosion of convulsive speed, Kinkaid whipped out his revolver and fired, point-blank! Not five feet from the extended muzzle of his gun was Duval's breast; but still he sat there, unscathed, smiling, his arms still lightly folded across his breast.

The horror-stricken eyes of the marshal turned down to the five shells which lay upon the table before him, then rose to Duval's pale face. He was still smiling.

Then he saw the other's hand disappear inside his coat and come forth again, bearing a revolver.

It was instinct that made the marshal half rise and stand like a crouched bear, ready to rush in. But some deep sense of dignity and of how men should meet their death made him, instead, stand suddenly erect, his hands gripped at his sides as the revolver swung up and leisurely covered him.

"That's the man-hunter, the man-killer, the bounty-taker," said Duval, sneering. "I took your gun from you, once. I could take your life from you now—but I'd rather let folks see what you're made of—and let you go. Get out!"

Once before, on a night of horror, the marshal had been sent in shame from that cabin; and now he went forth again with his head hanging on his chest. At the door, he gathered himself and, turning, cast a glance like that of a madman on Duval, then went slowly off through the darkness.

Old Henry, Duval himself, and Marian Lane remained with Charlie Nash.

It was Charlie who moved first and, saying nothing to anyone, poured himself a glass of water. His shaking hand spilled half of it on the floor; the rest he swallowed and then blundered out from the cabin and was gone.

"The horses, Henry!" said Duval huskily to Henry.

And Henry slipped away in turn, his eyes like those of men who have seen ghosts walk.

It left Duval and the girl alone, and the instant the others were away, he dropped his face in his hands and gripped the flesh hard with his fingers.

"Here," said a matter-of-fact voice, "some hot coffee. You didn't drink your first cup, David."

The fragrance of it and the heat rose up to his face.

"Very well," said he. "Thank you."

He had to make a pause between the words and speak very softly. Otherwise, he could not have been sure of the voice in which he spoke.

When he raised the cup, it chattered foolishly against his teeth; and he closed his eyes to shut out the face of Marian Lane who stood by, watching.

The heat, the stimulus, instantly helped him.

But still he dared not stir from his chair, for an odd sense of emptiness occupied his brain, and his body was weak! Weakness like a sensible thing ran in his nerves and in his blood.

"Why did you do it?" said Marian Lane.

She came close beside him.

"I know," said she. "You wanted to crush me with one last, gigantic act. You wanted to make me see that even the marshal was nothing to you.

She touched his hair.

"This is where his bullet clipped. Oh, David, David, to risk that for the sake of overwhelming poor Marian Lane, who keeps a country store! That was childish, David."

He found her with his hands, for he dared not open his eyes just now.

"Don't talk for a moment," said Duval. "Whatever you say is true. But I'm sick. I want to keep you here this moment. That's all!"

"So," said Duval at last, and stood up before her.

He was completely recovered, one would have said, from that instant of utter weakness, though still the girl watched him with a judicial air.

"Childish," he admitted. "That was it—plainly childish! But, after all, it worked, you see!"

"Not well enough to put you at ease, though," said she. "When I saw you fold your arms, I knew what you'd do, and I wanted to scream a warning, but it was much too late. I—there wasn't much left to me by that time!"

She smiled a wan smile.

"In every way," said Duval, "I was contemptible!"

"Hush," said the girl. "You saved a life! Is that contemptible?"

Then she added: "As for me, I deserved all the pain that came to me, I suppose."

She closed her eyes and shook her head a little to drive the picture of the horror away from her. "But now that it's over, it won't have to be repeated. And you're going away, David?"

"No," said he.

"Is it worth your while?" she asked him, half sadly and half curiously. "Is it worth your while to stay here, when you know that Dick Kinkaid will not stop with this one trial, but will surely come at you again? Is it worth while, for the sake of the little game that you're playing in Moose Creek?"

"How little is the game, Marian?" he asked.

"Only you can tell that, of course—Mr. Smith—Jones—Brown—or Van Astorgrand, or whatever your name is, David!"

"But don't you know," said Duval, "that you're carrying with you the proof of who I am?"

"The proof?" said she.

"The very name," he answered. "In the little chamois bag which our friend Kinkaid left with you."

Old Henry cried in a strange voice: "Are you tellin' her that? Are you tellin' her that?"

"Why, Henry," said Duval, "you heard me say before the world that this is the girl I love. This is she whom I intend to marry, if I can. Would you have her marry anything but a true name?"

"Only—only—" gasped Henry.

She had drawn from the bosom of her dress the small chamois sack, and holding it for a moment in both hands, she stared at Duval. He nodded at her. "Kinkaid has no right to ask you to keep that shut, if I ask you to open it!"

She, with a little faint cry of excitement, drew open the mouth of the bag and spilled upon the table's face—a creamy flow of big pearls!

Marian Lane looked up, at last, from the jewels, and stared straight at Duval.

"That wild, wild story you told me—" said she. "That fairy tale—that impossible thing—"

"It was all true, word for word!"

"And you weren't hiding yourself away from me?"

"I was laying the naked truth in your hands to see."

"But you didn't protest!"

"Why should I protest? I saw that you wouldn't believe a word that I had to say! I was right, I think."

She raised both hands to her face, and when, slowly, she lowered them, she was crimson with emotion.

"After that," she said, "it seems that everything you said may have had some truth in it. It wasn't quite all a game, then?"

"Do you think that any syllable was a game, Marian?"

"I don't know. I'm dizzy. I'm so dizzy, I can hardly see you at such a great distance!"

He came swiftly to her.

"I'm sure you see what it means," he said. "And that instead of being possibly an honorable Mr. Smith, or Jones, or Brown, I'm only David Castle, the jewel thief?"

Tears came up in her eyes.

"Stuff!" said she. "It means that you are *my* David. And there's no riddle at all!"

"You can bring the horses around, Henry," said Duval. "Then go down to Miss Lane's stable and get her own horse out, and ride it up the northwest trail. We won't be going very fast, and you can overtake us."

"But the store, and everything in it?" said she.

"You can settle that later on."

"And the scandal?"

"We'll put that right at the first minister's house. Because, if I'm to have you with me, do you think that I'll stay here another moment in danger of that juggernaut, Kinkaid? Shall I take one single step that will put me in the danger of the law, Marian? Not from this minute forward!"

"I have to go back for clothes!"

"You can be a boy for a day. I have clothes that will more than fit you!"

"But—"

"Shall I let you go back to Moose Creek, where they may be waiting and watching for you?"

He took her in his arms.

"Not a step without me. Not a step!"

"Wait!" said she. "I have to think—"

"Will you tell me that you love me, Marian, and do your thinking a little later on?"

"But there's so much to work out—I'll have to think for two, now!"

"Only answer me, first."

She stepped suddenly close to him, and stood tiptoe to bring her face closer to his.

"As if you didn't know," said she, "from the first moment, that I was only fighting against an overlord!"

24

Still, when the morning came, they were toiling upward and northward through the mountains. Their horses were tired. The riders were no less, and Marian Lane swayed a little in the saddle whenever her mount stumbled.

Duval called a halt, therefore, in the pink of the dawn, for they had found an ideal spot. The lodgepole pines formed a thin fencing around a shoulder of the mountain where the grass grew well for grazing, and where a small spring welled up into a white, sandy basin, then sent a silver trickle winding down the slope. Where the trees would throw their shadow, Duval and Henry made down two hasty beds of young boughs, and spread the blankets. One would stand watch while two slept, and Duval took the first turn, while Henry and the girl wrapped themselves in the blankets and were instantly asleep.

Duval, as he watched, threw back his shoulders, half smiling and half fierce, then hastily went back to the place where the girl slept. She was troubled in her sleep. He saw her frown and one hand moved outside the blanket as if in protest.

It troubled him more than he cared to say, and

when he saw her lips move, he kneeled to listen, ashamed of such eavesdropping, but humbly and hungrily intent on learning what her sorrow could be.

He only heard an indistinct murmur, but still he leaned above her, when she wakened and looked straight up at him, wide awake.

"It's your turn to sleep, David," she told him, and tried to sit up.

He held her back.

"Hush," said he. "You'll be waking Henry, for he's a light sleeper. You've hardly been here ten minutes asleep."

"An hour and a half. I'm made over by such a sleep!"

"Not that long."

"Look at your watch."

He saw that she was right.

"I've been coming by and looking at you from time to time," he said. "You've had a troubled sleep, my dear."

"I dreamed," said she, "that I was swimming towards a beach, and you were standing on it, and just as I came to the verge of the sand, just as I could put down a foot and touch it, a strong current took hold of me and drifted me far out to sea. You look actually frightened over my dream!"

"Because it gives me gloomy thoughts, my dear. Suppose that we love each other to the end, and are married, yet how many hours at the end of the years will we really have been together as we are now, on the mountainside here? We'll be like others, and leave happiness and love to cool their heels in a darkened room along with the poets on our shelves, while we give ourselves to the important business of the butcher and baker and candlestick-maker. And yet the mountains and the clouds and the wind and the morning are all full of joy simply because we love one another. And if—"

He stopped.

"I'm becoming romantic," said Duval. "The practical fact is that you must stop my talking by going to sleep again."

"I'm not going to sleep again," said she. "I'm going to lie awake, unless you'll let me get up and mount guard."

"A grand guard you'd be," said Duval.

"Are you going to make the old mistake and think that I have to be tied up in pink ribbon like a stick of candy for a baby?"

"You'll do as you please," said Duval.

"You'll find I can work," said Marian Lane. "Whatever you do, I'll find a way to help you."

"Of course you will," said Duval, "but you won't have to work to keep the wolf from the door. The poor old wolf will have to howl in the dim distance. Why, Marian, in that little chamois sack there's enough to banish him forever!"

She nodded.

"But not for us, I suppose?" said she.

"Not for us?" frowned Duval.

"You see," she explained, sitting up again, "I don't complain of what you did before, as long as we don't live on it now!"

"Wipe it all out?" said Duval, his breath taken. "Millions are what you're talking about! Millions, child!"

Then he added, almost roughly: "It's better to let me worry about how the money is made. Now, you go back to sleep."

She did not argue or protest, but lay back again in the bed of boughs with the faintest of frowns, and as she lay looking up at him, and past him, he saw her hand make the same slight motion of protest which he had watched in her sleep.

Duval was instantly on his knees beside her.

"You're right!" he said. "And I'm an ass. To think that I could keep you with stolen goods! To be fool enough to think that! It goes back to the right owner, and it goes at once. Here, take the stuff. I won't be tempted with the beauties!"

She took them.

"I wanted to say—" she said, and paused.

"Yes," said Duval.

She took his hand and pressed it.

"I wondered how hard it would be, but if this is so easy, I'll never have another thing to ask of you, David. Do you believe that?"

"With all my heart."

"And—" said she.

"Yes?" murmured Duval, after a moment.

But her hand gradually relaxed and fell away from his, and when he looked down at her again, he saw that she was profoundly asleep and smiling in her slumber.

It was much later when she wakened again. The cracking of a twig underfoot had roused her, and as she sat up, blinking, she saw old Henry standing on the meadow looking anxiously about him on all sides.

When he saw that she was awake he said eagerly: "Did he tell you where he was going?"

"No," said the girl. "Not a word. Going? David? He's not gone, Henry!"

The old man pointed.

"There's the other two hosses. Where's Cherry?"

She was on her feet by this time, all sleep startled from her mind.

And then Henry stretched out his long arm and pointed down the valley.

"Is that David coming back?" he asked.

She got her glasses out of her pack. Strong Zeiss field glasses, they picked up distant objects with wonderful detail. And when she focused them on the far-off rider, it was to exclaim immediately: "A gray horse, that one—not Cherry. Looks like a big horse and a big man—only I can't be sure."

"A gray horse? Like Kinkaid's?" asked Henry.

She lowered the glasses to give Henry one keen glance. Then she raised them again and spoke with them at her eyes.

"Now that you've given me the idea, it seems to me that you may be right. A big man on a large gray horse—riding hard—I can see the way he rounds the curves in the trail. Who else would be coming up against the grade so hard and fast? Dick Kinkaid!"

She lowered the glasses and added: "David has seen him long ago. He's gone down to meet Kinkaid!"

She passed the glasses to Henry.

"You try to find him, will you?"

Then she leaned one hand against the tree trunk and waited, her eyes closed, as the old man searched the upper ravine.

Suddenly he cried out: "I've got him! I see him now!"

"Are you sure?"

"I know Cherry's stride even at this distance! Look, look!"

She ran to him and snatched the glasses away.

"Look down into the lower canyon," said Henry, uselessly pointing. "There where the boulder nest begins. You'll see Cherry galloping, and who but him would be ridin' her?"

She found him almost at once.

"Get my horse!" she cried to Henry, still with the glasses glued to her eyes.

"It's too late to do no good," said Henry with great decision. "There ain't any use. Because he'll be sure to crash agin Kinkaid in another few seconds—now, maybe?"

"He's out from the rocks!" said the girl. "They're riding straight at each other! They're meeting near a grove of trees—pines, I think—they—"

Her voice choked away, then she began again, chattering the words out rapidly.

"I thought he was down, but he'd only slipped down alongside his horse, I suppose—that old Indian trick! And now he's up again. I thought I saw the glint of the sun on the guns! I can't be sure—they've closed! They're both down—Henry, Henry, they're both down, and Dick Kinkaid has those huge hands on David!"

"Then God help Kinkaid's unlucky soul!" said Henry solemnly, "because he ain't gunna live to talk about this day! What's happenin' now?"

"They've rolled into the shade of the trees, and I can't see anything. Get my horse—my horse! Henry, Henry! Be quick!"

At last the saddle and bridle were on. He gave her a leg up, and she dashed the pony down the hillside, like water leaping with full head, swerving around big boulders, dodging among the trees.

Never was there madder riding than that which

took Marian Lane down to the bottom of the lower ravine. For she told herself that God would not let her have such happiness as that which had been in touch of her hand; Duval was dead; it must be so, and therefore she rode wildly, not caring greatly what came of her in that perilous descent.

So she reached the lower and level footing, with the mustang stretched out at full gallop, and came plunging on to the view of the pines under whose shadow she had watched Duval disappear.

And then she saw a man seated on a rock at the edge of the woods, and waving a hat at her.

Duval!

She came closer, and made sure that it was he. But why did he remain there, seated?

On and on rushed the mustang, and now she could tell a vitally good reason, for blood ran down one side of his face, and blood soaked his torn and ragged shirt, and blood streaked his trousers, also.

She was out of the saddle with a leap, like a man, and there was David smiling up at her with perfect peace in his face.

"Davie, Davie, Davie!" sobbed the girl. "He's killed you!"

"He wouldn't say so, if you asked him," said Duval, calmly. "He's gone back toward Moose Creek a rather sick fellow, Marian. When Henry comes jogging along, we'll send him after Kinkaid to see that the pieces get home, safely. Dead? I'll live to be a thousand, if I'm never sicker than I am now!"

His head drooped back against the tree trunk behind him, however, as he spoke; it was instantly supported in the crook of her arm, and she heard a rapid murmur saying: "I'll live, Marian. No fear of that, my dear, but work fast! The life is soaking out of me. Fast, fast!"

And when Henry came, he found Duval with eyes closed, senseless, and the girl working white-lipped, stern, with determination.

Between them they closed the wounds with bandages.

And long after, Duval opened his eyes and gritted his teeth as he felt the binding power that was on his hurts. He mastered himself at once, and was able to smile wanly up at Marian Lane.

"He was down and out, the cur," said Duval. "And he gave in. And after that, he came at me again when my head was turned. He came like a blind beast—and I can thank God for the blindness, or I wouldn't be living in your hands, my dear! But at last he was done for. He backed away from me, Marian, and ran for his horse—and he's ridden out of our lives forever. He'll ride other trails, but never the trail that leads to me again!"

This is the history of David Duval as Moose Creek knew it, and a great deal more, in some respects, than all of Moose Creek knew.

As for David and his wife, they never came back to the little town again.

It was said that he was ill for a long time in the mountains, until she and Henry had nursed him back to some shadow of his old strength, and then they resumed their journey north and west to a new land, and to a new life.

Once a rumor came back to Moose Creek from a wanderer who spoke of a little village in Maryland, a shining sweep of river, wide meadows green as lawns, a spacious grove, a house on a hill, and a happy face at a window that looked strangely like the face of Marian Lane, not a whit older than she had been in the former days.

But there was never any confirmation of this rumor, and now Duval and Marian Lane have both joined the ghostly procession of legendary forms which ride across the imagination of the West.

WESTERNS

Nelson Nye

☐ 14199	**DEATH VALLEY SLIM** $1.95	
☐ 30798	**GUN FEUD AT TIEDOWN/ROGUES RENDEZVOUS** $2.25	
☐ 37343	**IRON HAND** $1.95	
☐ 80576	**THEIF RIVER** $1.95	
☐ 52041	**THE MARSHAL OF PIOCHE** $1.95	
☐ 58376	**THE NO-GUN FIGHTER** $1.95	

Double Westerns

☐ 04731 **BANCROFT'S BANCO/SEVEN SIX-GUNNERS** $2.25

Available wherever paperbacks are sold or use this coupon.

C ACE CHARTER BOOKS
P.O. Box 400, Kirkwood, N.Y. 13795

Please send me the titles checked above. I enclose $_____.
Include $1.00 per copy for postage and handling. Send check or money order only. New York State residents please add sales tax.

NAME_____

ADDRESS_____

CITY_____ STATE_____ ZIP_____

C-01